# THE PORTAL

## HOLLY HUDSPETH

The Portal

Book Five in The Skyy Huntington Series

All rights reserved

Copyright © 2016 Holly Hudspeth

Cover art by Rebecca Frank

Publisher: Holly Hudspeth

Dedicated to all of the amazing author friends I have met on this crazy writing adventure! A HUGE thank you to Emily Reese, and James Martinez, who helped me get this book ready to release! Miracle Austin…so glad our paths crossed. You are the sweetest, kindest person I know. Thank you to all of you, for keeping me motivated, and for being there for me!

Books by Holly Hudspeth:

The Lie – Book One in the Skyy Huntington Series

The Countess – Book Two in the Skyy Huntington Series

The Pursuit – Book Three in the Skyy Huntington Series

Guided by Moonlight – Lucius' Story – Book Four in the Skyy Huntington Series

The Portal – Book Five in the Skyy Huntington Series

Table of Contents

# Chapter 1

Two weeks had passed since the wedding. Aiden took me on a wonderful honeymoon, where we ravished each other almost non-stop. We had taken up residence at the castle in Scotland again, and for a very brief time I thought that we might just have some peace for a while.

Though we had finally defeated Elizabeth Bathory, we still were on the lookout for Jackson Ripleigh, also known as the famous serial killer, Jack the Ripper. While he was nowhere near as powerful as Bathory had been, he was still a psychopath who needed to be stopped. Ridley informed us that he may very well be in New Orleans, due to recent news reports. The murders fit his style, and had popped up suddenly, right around the same time that he disappeared from London.

So here we were, back in the United States much to my delight, in The Big Easy. Don't get me wrong, I love the castle in Scotland, and I loved seeing parts of Europe. But, for the most part I was not visiting those locations under the best of terms. There is nothing like being back home, around the things that are familiar to you.

Ridley and I got the Divine Assassins permission to rent a house in New Orleans, even though we could teleport anywhere we needed to go, we thought it was best to have a base of operations locally as well. We had been here two days, and it was my first time in the city. I can't say I was really enjoying it either. Being a vampire now, all of my senses were heightened, and the city stinks...literally. The first few times we ventured out into the French Quarter, where the murders had taken place, I was taken aback by the smell of beer, food, vomit, trash, and even urine that wafted on the air. This was a party city, and it showed.

Don't get me wrong, there is a certain charm about New Orleans, but you have to be able to overlook all the crime and filth to see it. Beautiful buildings and architecture, and lots of history are all around you. And me being the person who met my husband in a graveyard, found that some of their cemeteries were absolutely beautiful too. They were mostly oven tombs; all of them were above ground, because the earth is so spongy that bodies can easily just float back up after they are buried. Apparently the city had some issues with this back in the old days, and I think everyone can agree that above ground tombs are preferable to dead bodies floating in the streets!

Ridley and I were out getting acquainted with the city and its layout those first two days we were there, and I would teleport back to Scotland to see Aiden a few times a day. I really hated being away from him, especially since we were newlyweds. Our whole relationship has been an adventure, and just when I thought we had some breathing room to really enjoy each other, I had to head to New Orleans.

We had already scouted the three murder scenes that made headlines. The locals that lived in the area were all scared. People came to the city from all over the world to party, and of course there was crime, but these murders really shocked the community. When someone is ripped to pieces and then rearranged, people kind of take notice to that.

The other thing that was glaringly obvious was that we were not alone here. There were a *lot* of other vampires. There were several little shops and boutiques that catered to the occult scattered around the French Quarter, that sold everything from voodoo dolls, to fake vampire fangs…but these vampires were real. And they walked around at night with nothing to hide. You see a lot of weird people on Bourbon Street, so I am not sure why this shocked me as much as it did, but these vampires didn't even try to hide the fact that they were vampires. Mortals probably thought it was just fake fangs and cool special effects contacts, but to me they stood out like a sore thumb.

Another thing we soon found out about, is that there is a huge underground vampire culture here, with both humans pretending to be vampires, and actual vampires preying on those humans who think they are role playing with other humans. We found a "by invite only" club last night that is run by real vampires. They let humans come in there to role play, and while the majority of the people in there were actual humans, there were quite a few vampires in there as well. It was quite sad to see all the humans with their fake fangs and white makeup on, trying to act like what they imagine a real vampire would look like. As if we sit around all day in black pleather, wearing spiked collars and black fingernail polish.

And don't even get me started on how unsafe it is to share blood from human to human. But there were plenty of people in the club cutting themselves and letting their "vampire" lick from the wound. I also found myself struggling to keep my own blood lust in check, though thankfully the club serves actual blood to its real vampire customers under the guise of a Bloody Mary. Ridley was very uncomfortable, and was approached by several young goth girls in their twenties. He politely declined, and I took it upon myself to tell anyone else who came up to him that he was my blood slave. That shut them up really quick.

Though we found out a lot about New Orleans and its vampire underground, we had not come across Jack. Most of the real vampires we encountered were not very friendly, but the few I could talk to had not seen anyone fitting his description around town.

We were now coming into the third night in the city, and decided to hang out in Jackson Square for a few hours. Two of the murders had taken place in the vicinity of the Square, so it wasn't a bad place to start. In the span of an hour, I counted eight real vampires that walked by us. The ninth one was sitting not too far away from us, drinking from a human in public! It looked as though he was kissing her neck, but I could smell the blood, and hear the victim's heart racing as he sucked from her vein. She seemed to be enjoying it though, and was in no distress, and even though it bothered me that this vampire was so brazen in public, I decided it wasn't my business and left it alone.

What was worse is that because I knew other vampires were around and could hear us, we couldn't talk about our case, Jack, Bathory, or anything like that out loud. You never know who could be listening, and since we knew for a fact that Bathory had a residence at one point in this city, some of her vampires could very well be skulking around here.

Ridley and I became experts at having conversations either written down on a pad of paper, or typing them out on our phones. Our main goal here was to scout things out. If we found something, the Divine Assassins, and my vampire family, would be here in an instant. We didn't want to call too much attention to ourselves until then.

The Divine Assassins, well most of them anyway, really did not like working so closely with the vampires. But that was tough shit for them, since without the help of my friends, we probably wouldn't have been able to do half the stuff we'd accomplished so far. As much as it killed them to admit it, the vampires and the Divine Assassins made a nice, rounded out team.

Ridley was one of the exceptions. He had been a Divine Assassin as long as he could remember. His dad was in the Order as well, but his mom and sister had suffered a terrible fate at the hands of Bathory. His reasons for being a Divine Assassin were personal, just as much as professional. He and I hit it off from the get-go, though he was very shocked to find out I willingly wanted to become a vampire. My vampire family and I have quickly grown on him though, and I consider him to be not only my partner, but someone I can trust and call a friend.

I could tell that he was uncomfortable in this city of vampires. His eyes were shifting back and forth non-stop looking for any possible threats. We hung out in Jackson Square for quite some time. The smells, once again, were noxious to me. There were fortune tellers who read palms and tarot that burned disgusting smelling incense that was enough to choke me. Booze, body odor, food…even the smell of the Mississippi river, and the powdered sugar from the beignets at Café Du Monde were making me feel sick.

Ridley was a nervous wreck, his foot tapping on the ground with lightning speed. He had on his usual dweeb-wear; a button up shirt with every single button done, khaki dress pants with a belt that was cinched to the extreme, and his brown hair meticulously parted to one side and slicked down. If anything was going to give us away, it was him sticking out in the crowd.

"Hey, what do you think about a little shopping spree?" I asked him, as I poked him on the shoulder playfully.

He pushed his glasses up onto the bridge of his nose, and looked at me. "You want to go shopping?" he replied, thinking that I meant shopping for me. "It's kind of late for that, isn't it?"

"Nah. This city never sleeps. It's only ten at night. I think I saw a cool shop a few blocks over. Whatcha think?" I said, as I stood up, dusting my pants off.

"Umm. Alright, I guess. Not like much else is going on," Ridley replied, as he stood up with me. He gathered up our backpacks, I grabbed my purse, and we headed over to a little goth boutique I scoped out on the first day.

The clothes in here were the complete opposite of anything Ridley would ever wear, which was the whole point. We stepped into the shop, and I cringed at the loud music blaring on the speakers. Ridley glanced around the store uncertainly, taking it all in.

"So, let's get you some new clothes for while we're in town. What's your favorite color? What size pants and shirt do you wear?" I questioned him. He was tall and slender, and I wasn't going to make him wear anything too extreme, but at least something that looked casual-fun.

Ridley's eyes almost popped out of his head. "What do you mean, what size pants do I wear?! I wouldn't be caught dead in anything here, Skyy!" he exclaimed, a little too loudly. One of the clerks was making her way over to us to greet us, and heard his confession. She just smiled at us, and introduced herself.

"Hi, I'm Aimee. All shirts are buy one, get one half price. And shoes are all fifty percent off. I take it this is your first time in here, cutie?" she said, as she flirted with Ridley. She was cute, if not for the facial jewelry and dyed green hair.

Ridley stuttered on his words, still shocked that we were in here to shop for him, no doubt. "Umm, uhhh. Yes, this is my first time in here. Skyy, can I talk to you for a moment?" he asked, looking at me with pure panic on his face.

Aimee laughed, and told us that she'd be up front if we needed her for anything before walking off. "I know what you're going to say, Ridley. Save your breath. We're getting you some more stylish clothes. I need you to fit in…to blend in. See where I am going with this?" I asked him, putting emphasis on blending in.

"You're too easy to spot in a crowd," I whispered. "What you have on is fine for working back at the office, but this is the 21st century. You're young and hot, you might as well dress like it!" I added, poking him in the ribs with my elbow and flashing him a smile.

He knew he was defeated, and didn't even put up an argument. "Young and hot. Pffft," he mocked me. "Fine, let's try on some clothes. I know you won't stop bugging me until I do," he said, as he motioned for me to lead the way.

I clapped my hands, and did a little dance before heading off to the racks of clothing. I scoured the racks, grabbing a bunch of t-shirts and some casual dress up shirts, and handed them to Aimee to put in a dressing room. Then we headed to the pants. I snatched up some basic jeans, and a few pairs of shorts, a couple of dressier pants, as well as a pair of black goth pants with chains and studs all over them. These would be good to wear in the underground vampire club. He'd blend right in.

Ridley went into the changing room reluctantly, but didn't voice his disapproval. I made him show me everything he was trying on, and I was shocked when he first came out. He had a cute face, even with all of his dweeb-wear, but I really never realized just how cute until I saw him in normal clothes. His hair had gotten ruffled from putting on the shirt, and for once he looked like a normal, twenty-something guy.

I exhaled the breath I had not realized I'd been holding. "Wow. You look awesome, Ridley! You sure clean up nice!" I exclaimed, as I stood up and made him spin around.

"I *was* cleaned up nice," he said, sarcastically. I ignored his comment, and just rolled my eyes as I continued to look him over. Aimee even came over to admire the new look.

"Lookin' good!" she said, flirting with him again. I could see him blush, as he wasn't used to all this attention, and especially from females. Ridley went back into the changing room and tried on all of the clothing I had picked out for him. None of it, with the exception of the goth pants, was too extreme, and he looked great in everything.

But when he finally tried on the goth pants, it was hard for me not to laugh at him. "I'm not coming out there, Skyy! No way in hell!" he exclaimed from behind the door.

I giggled, and replied, "Aww, come on Ridley. Just let me see!"

"No. Way." he replied, firmly.

"Don't make me come in there to look!" I shot back at him.

The dressing room door opened, and nothing but his head peeped out. "These look ridiculous on me, Skyy! Are you crazy? I'm not wearing these things!"

The fact that I was already laughing picturing what he looked like in the pants wasn't helping. "Come on out Ridley, just for a second. Humor me, please?"

He sighed loudly and dramatically. "You owe me. Big time," he growled, as he stepped out of the dressing room. The pants were ridiculous on him, that was for sure. They were your typical goth pants; huge legs, tons of chains and studs, and the foot holes were the size of basketball hoops. He stood there with his hands in the pockets looking at the ground.

At this point I was laughing so hard I almost fell off the bench outside the dressing room. I had to catch my breath before speaking. "Ridley, I know they are something you would never wear in a million years, but they will be perfect for the club," I emphasized. "Think about it, please?" I encouraged him.

He sighed as he stared off towards the wall like a pouty teenager, then his eyes lit up. "Alright, make you a deal. You make me wear these stupid pants, and I get to pick out your outfit for the club. Fair?"

I looked over to where his eyes were, and saw a wall of S&M type women's clothing. Lots of latex, corsets, fishnet, and see-thru stuff. Ridley was the one laughing now, and I just sighed. "Fine, fine. I guess that's fair," I replied, knowing that the only way I'd get him to buy any of these clothes was if I walked out of here in something just as ridiculous.

He picked out a black latex cat suit for me, and thank God I had a body that could rock it, because it hugged EVERY single curve of my body. Some knee-high boots with heels that were the most uncomfortable things on the planet to walk in, and a cute belt finished the look off. I would be just as uncomfortable as he was in the damn things, not to mention I never wear heels, so walking on the uneven streets of the French Quarter should turn out to be a blast.

I bought everything I had picked out for Ridley, as well as a few new pairs of shoes for him, and a shirt to go with his new goth pants. Now, maybe if I could convince him to style his hair better, he'd be a full package.

As we were checking out, Aimee asked us if we were local. I shook my head no as I dug in my purse for my credit card. "No, we're from Scotland," I replied…sort of telling the truth.

Her eyes lit up with that, and she looked Ridley over once more. "Wow! Scotland! You don't have the cute accents though," she mentioned as she continued to ring us up.

"My husband does. He was born and raised there," I answered her.

At the mention of me having a husband, her eyes lit up even more at the discovery that Ridley was potentially single. "That's so cool. I'd love to go to Scotland someday," she said.

We had bought a ton of clothes and shoes, and there was no way we would be able to carry this stuff around, so I asked her if we could go back and get our car to pick the items up in about a half hour.

"Sure! We don't close until midnight. Hey, if you guys are wanting to go out later, there is a really cool underground club I can get you into," she replied cheerfully.

"Okay, we'll talk about it while we go get the car," I answered her as I handed her my credit card. After settling the bill, we walked to where our rental car was parked and hopped in.

"What do you think about this club she is inviting us to?" I asked Ridley.

He shrugged and answered, "Are you making me wear those stupid pants? If so, the answer is no."

I burst out laughing. "We can wear normal clothes tonight. I'd like to go back to the vampire club tomorrow night, though you never know what we might run into tonight. I think we should go," I said, as I clicked my seatbelt.

"I will follow your lead, Skyy. You know more about this scene than I do," Ridley replied, as we pulled out of the parking lot and headed to the clothing store.

Aimee had all of our bags ready to go by the time we pulled up to the curb. She gladly helped us load them into the trunk and the backseat. Once that was settled I let her know we'd be interested in checking out her underground club.

"What kind of club is it?" I questioned.

"Oh, they play a lot of techno, and have some really cool guest DJ's there. It's pretty laid back, but it doesn't open until midnight, and stays open until ten in the morning," she replied, happily.

"Okay, that sounds fun. Do we need to meet you outside to get in, or how does it work?"

"Either way. I'll be there with a few girlfriends tonight; we can meet you outside. How about twelve-thirty? I have to close up here at midnight, and it is just a few streets over. Here is the address," she said, as she jotted down the directions on the back of my receipt.

"We'll see you there," I told her, as we hopped back in the car. Ridley actually gave her a little smile and a wave goodbye. Once we were on the road, I informed him we were going to the house to get him changed.

All I got in response was a loud sigh from him. Our rental house wasn't too far from the French Quarter, and we made it there pretty fast. After lugging all the bags inside, I began to sort through all of his new duds, taking the tags off as I made piles from the shirts, pants, and shorts. As I did so, I pointed at Ridley and told him, "*You*, sir, are going to take a quick shower. And then we're going to do something with your hair."

His mouth opened to object, but before he could, I added in, "No arguing. Go!" I watched in amusement as he skulked off to the bathroom knowing it was a battle he wouldn't win. I picked out a casual pair of jeans, and a t-shirt that had a comic book hero on the front of it, along with a pair of Vans shoes. He'd blend in and look like a normal guy.

I tossed the clothing onto the bed in his room, then shouted out to him to get dressed and let me know when he was done. About ten minutes later, the new and improved Ridley emerged from his room. Smiling at him, I nodded my head in approval. "You look great, Ridley. Let's do your hair," I told him, as I shuffled him into the bathroom again.

"Stay here a sec," I said, as I ran to my bathroom to grab some mousse, hair gel, and hair spray. Back in his bathroom, I played around with his brown hair until I got the desired look. I messed it up a little, spiking certain pieces up here and there a bit. A few spritzes of hairspray, which Ridley didn't like at all, and he was done.

He put his glasses back on, and stared at himself in the mirror. I was grinning from ear to ear. It didn't even look like the same guy! "I look...weird," was all he said.

"You look hot!" I encouraged him. It wasn't a lie...he actually did look quite handsome.

"I smell like a girl with this crap in my hair," he countered.

"Well, don't you have some cologne or something?" I asked him, as I put my hands on my hips.

He shook his head no. Of course he didn't...it was Ridley the computer nerd we were talking about here.

I sighed out loud. But there was a solution to this problem. "Stay here!" I told him as I opened up a portal to my castle in Scotland. Moments later I emerged in another country on the other side of the world. Rushing over to the side of the castle where Aiden's offices were, I called out to my husband, "Babe?! You home?"

Within a split second Aiden appeared and embraced me in his arms. Smiling at him, I planted a kiss on his lips. He returned it gladly, and then looked me in the eyes at arm's length. "Is everything ok, milady?" he asked me with worry. I showed up with no notice...not that he minded, but he worried about me pretty much all of the time.

I placed my hand on his cheek and assured him everything was fine. His light green eyes were beginning to glow with the excitement of seeing his wife. "Yes, darling. Everything is fine. I gave Ridley a make-over, and I need to borrow some cologne from you if that's ok?"

Aiden chuckled at the news. "A make-over? The poor guy...I can only imagine what you did to him," he said.

I swatted him on his arm gently. "Hey! I am not going to turn into your mother, don't worry. He needed a little...help...is all. He sticks out like a sore thumb in New Orleans. We can't be going into underground vampire clubs with him dressed like a computer nerd," I said, defending myself.

"That is true. His fashion sense isn't very good, I'll admit. Let's go upstairs and you can pick out a cologne for him. Where are you going this evening?" he inquired, as we jetted up the stairs.

Opening the bottles of cologne he had on his dresser and sniffing them, I replied, "Not sure. We met a cashier at the clothing store who is getting us into some secret nightclub. Figure it's worth a shot. I don't know the city well enough yet, but tomorrow night we'll hit the vampire club again."

Aiden was rubbing my shoulders as I inspected the bottles, which quickly led to him gently kissing my neck, which then quickly progressed to him nipping my neck and licking up blood. I placed the bottle in my hand on the dresser, and turned around to face him. He placed his bloodied lips to mine, igniting a passionate kiss.

The bloody kiss turned into ten minutes of love-making and nipping, followed by my urgent need to drink blood. Three cups later, I was back at the dresser sniffing bottles once more. Picking out a no-doubt expensive bottle of cologne from Aiden's collection, I stuffed it into the back pocket of my jeans.

Aiden came up behind me once more, this time gathering up my long auburn hair into his hands and playing with it. "You guys want some company tonight?" he asked, flashing his perfect smile at me in the mirror.

"Thought you'd never ask," I replied, happy to have my husband along with us tonight.

He quickly changed into some designer jeans, and a polo shirt, and we were off through the portal back to New Orleans. The whole trip took about twenty-five minutes, but Ridley was used to this by now. Ever since the wedding, I would do several "be right back" errands a day, just as an excuse to see my husband. I tossed him the cologne out of my back pocket, and he thanked Aiden for letting him borrow it.

"No problem, Ridley. You're looking sharp. Skyy told me she took you shopping tonight," he said, as he greeted him with a smile and a handshake.

"Did she add in it was an unwilling shopping trip?" he chuckled.

Aiden laughed with him and added, "I've learned it's best to not argue with her, and just go along with whatever the plan is. Saves you the hassle in the long run."

"Ain't that the truth," Ridley replied.

"If you boys don't mind; I am going to get cleaned up. We only have about a half hour until we are supposed to meet Aimee outside the club. Be back in a few," I told them, as I excused myself to the other room.

Not knowing what kind of club this was other than "laid back" I put on a short black skirt, and a silver sequined dress top that was low cut in the front, and pretty much bare in the back. I didn't have much time to do anything fancy with my hair, so I just brushed it out and ran a flat iron through it. A touch of makeup, some cute ankle boots, and I was good to go. Popping in a fresh pair of my special contacts that Ridley had made for me to hide my crazy purple eyes was the final touch before I walked out the door.

Having to drive cars around in a congested city when we could portal was annoying. But somehow we made it there right at twelve-thirty. Aimee was excited to see us, but mostly to see Ridley, and introduced us to her two friends. They all seemed friendly enough, and I introduced them to Aiden. I could see the drool beginning to form as he spoke with his adorable Scottish accent.

We were ushered in through the backdoor of the club, which was filled to the brim with people already. Loud techno music was pumping on the speakers, and the dancefloor was filled. It was hot and humid inside, as expected, and the stench once again assaulted my nostrils. There were fog machines, and lots of lighting effects, as well as a stage area, and three bars. A narrow staircase led up to a smaller, more relaxed second floor that had on ambient music. I assumed this was where the stoners hung out, as the couches were filled with people who were in a zombie-like state.

Our group went back downstairs after Aimee showed us around, and she walked behind the bar to find someone. Moments later, she came back with a guy in his mid-forties who escorted us to a table tucked into the corner of the room.

It wrapped around the sides and corner of the room comfortably, and there was room for everyone around it. The plush velvet cushioning on it was comfy, and I snuggled into Aiden's side as the girls ordered drinks. I noticed that Aimee snuck in beside Ridley, who was off to my right side. The bartender came back shortly with a tray full of shots, and after my last experience with alcohol as a vampire, I knew it was a waste of money, but we each took one anyway.

Aimee insisted that Ridley have one too, and I wasn't entirely sure, but wondered if this might be the first time he'd ever had a drink. We could tell he was uncomfortable as hell, but he went along with it anyway. As the girls kept chatting and ordering more shots, I was scanning the club for anyone odd or out of place.

When we walked in earlier, I immediately noticed two different tables of vampires on opposite sides of the club. There were about ten vampires at each table. They all noticed Aiden and I as well, and glared at us with unfriendly faces. As far as I could tell, they were the only vampires in the club.

Aiden was softly caressing my bare shoulder with the tips of his fingers as we gazed around the club. I was so happy that he was here with me tonight, and felt safer with him by my side. Ridley, now about four shots deep, was finally smiling. The alcohol was kicking in, and I could tell he was loosening up. Normally I would be happy about that, but I needed him to be alert and on his game tonight in case something happened.

Aimee and her friends slid out from behind the table a few moments later. "You want to dance, Ridley?" she asked him shyly, as she offered him her hand. He glanced at me for approval, and I nodded to him. As he walked by me, I whispered, "Stay close," to him, and he got the idea.

Watching Ridley attempt to dance was probably one of the funniest things I have ever witnessed in my life. He had zero rhythm. Aimee was a good sport, she could tell he lacked any coordination too, and was trying to teach him some dance moves.

They were on the dancefloor for quite some time, before I noticed a brawl about to break out over at the vampire table. The vampires from across the club were over at the other vampires table, and they were out for blood. They were speaking in Cajun-French, and although I had read books and consumed some learning potions on the language, they were hard to understand. One word I definitely could make out though, was *Bathory*. My ears perked up when I heard her name mentioned, and without trying to look too interested, I listened in for more of the conversation.

The fight quickly escalated into an all-out fist fight, and the whole club was now staring at the vampires. I was curious to see how this would play out, since we were mostly among humans in here. The bartender that had escorted us to our seats pushed his way through the crowd of people, and held up a spray bottle in his hands. I could not see what was in the bottle, but he quickly got their attention.

"Hey! That's enough of your shit! Take your fight outside, or you'll get what I gave you last time," he informed them, holding up the spray bottle. The vampires all glared at him, and some of them gathered their things and left. I made a mental note of what the vampire looked like that was using Bathory's name. It would be too obvious for us to follow them out of here and track them, and without the rest of my Divine Assassins or my vampire family with me, it would probably end bad for the three of us. So we let them walk out.

Whatever was in that bottle was something the vampires were scared of…probably silver of some kind, and the bartender knew exactly what they were. It had me intrigued for sure, and I debated on approaching him and asking him about it. Aimee, Ridley, and her two friends all came back and sat down. "Wow, that was exciting, huh!?" she exclaimed.

I nodded at her, and smiled. After some small talk, I asked her what the bartenders name was, and she told me it was Pierce. Thanking her, I excused myself and walked over to his section of the bar. "Hi there, I am over at the table with Aimee," I introduced myself, smiling.

He did not return the smile, but instead said, "I know what you are, and if you mean to cause trouble here in my club, you'll get the same treatment the others did."

Confusion crossed my face, and he could tell that I was not from around here. "I'm sorry I'm being so harsh. Have had too many of your kind come in my place and destroy it over Coven feuds. Aimee is my little cousin, I'm curious what you and your friends are wanting with her," he said, bluntly.

"Umm, actually we are new in town. We met her tonight at the clothing shop. I was in there helping my friend get some new clothes. She seemed to take a fancy to him, and invited us here," I replied, honestly.

He nodded his head in the direction of Aiden, "So who's the other vamp with you then?"

I glanced over at Aiden and waved to him. He smiled back at me, and did his best to pretend that he wasn't keeping a close eye on me. "That is my husband, Aiden. Ridley is the one with Aimee," I explained.

"So what are two vampires doing with a human in here tonight, if not to cause trouble?" he inquired. He was a tall man, who had a dark black beard and moustache, dark eyes, and a decent build. Dressed in all black as well, I could easily picture him riding a motorcycle.

"Well, I barely know you but I understand your concern for your establishment. Ridley is a friend and colleague of mine. We aren't looking for any trouble at all, actually," I said, trying not to be offended by his rudeness.

His eyes narrowed a bit as he continued his examination. "What Coven are you with?" he shot back.

"We aren't with any coven. My husband, and a handful of others stick together, but we are not affiliated with any coven or group. Is there something we should be aware of here in the city? As I said, we are brand new to town," I asked, concerned for his paranoia.

"I have never met a vampire without a coven before," he said, ignoring my question and examining me further.

"Well, I can assure you me and my family are not here to cause trouble. Plenty of vampires are not part of covens. We like to stick together, and keep things small," I answered.

"There are droves of vamps here in New Orleans. All out for themselves. At least seven different covens, all at war with each other. You'll have to forgive me and my questions, I don't have good experiences with your kind. And with word of one of the most powerful vamps being back in town, things will only get worse. Just don't get my cousin Aimee involved in this shit, that's all I ask," Pierce said, finally letting his guard down.

"Who is back in town, if you don't mind me asking?"

"I'm sure you've heard of her. Everyone has…Bathory," was his reply. My stomach sank at the mention of her name. We were in town for Jack the Ripper…I killed Bathory with my own hands, and was positive she was dead.

I guess the shock showed on my face, since Pierce asked, "See, everyone knows who she is. Nothing but trouble. If I were you, I'd consider a new place to live, and get out of New Orleans,"

"Thanks for talking with me Pierce. We might see you again soon, and I promise we won't get Aimee involved in any of this. Does she know…you know, about…vampires and such too?" I asked.

He shook his head no. "Nope, and I hope it stays that way. She is a good kid," he replied.

After my chat with Pierce, I told Ridley that we needed to get going. A quick phone number exchange with Aimee, and we were all back in the car on the way back to our rental house. "We've got SERIOUS problems, guys," I said, once we were outside of the French Quarter.

# Chapter 2

Aiden heard the entire conversation I had with Pierce, but Ridley hadn't. He was half drunk from the shots that Aimee and her friends insisted he drink, but he sobered up as best he could at the devastating news.

"If this is true, we are back at stage one again. She must have had a phylactery somewhere we didn't know about," I stated in disgust. Aiden was driving, and I was in the passenger seat of the rental car, twirling my long hair around my index finger like crazy. We had enough on our hands, and now this.

Aiden rested his hand just above my knee to comfort me. "I got a message from Lucius when you were at the bar. He and Flavia were planning on heading this way. They were in Russia, and are bringing their new friend Sergei with them. So at least they will be here soon enough, and I can call Mother and inform her. I am sure they can be ready to leave at a moment's notice as well. When will your grandfather be sending out more Divine Assassins?" he inquired.

I shrugged my shoulders, "No idea. As far as they knew up until this moment, we were just scouting the area for Jack. As soon as we get back to the house I will let them know we need to form a plan for Bathory."

"I wonder if Jack knows she is here in New Orleans as well. After their last encounter, I'd imagine Bathory is pretty pissed off at him," Ridley chimed in from the backseat.

The last time Jack and Bathory were together, he had tricked her and it ended up getting her killed. Or…at least that is what we thought. "Well, it won't take him long to find out with all the vampires here blabbing it around town. I wouldn't imagine Jack would be hanging out at club's other vampires frequent though, seeing that is he a lone-wolf," I replied.

"We might miss the opportunity to get to him if he finds out Bathory is here. He'll take off if he thinks he is in danger," Aiden said.

Nodding my head, I replied, "I know. But between the two, Bathory is the bigger threat. If she has been reincarnated she'll be weak, but she has powerful vampires and the dark fae behind her, and it won't take her long to get back on her feet. Jack is a creature of habit, and we'll find him again eventually if he does flee...but for now let's keep our fingers crossed that he stays in New Orleans for the time being."

We pulled up to our rental house. I knew from this point on that Aiden would not leave my side. If there was even a suggestion that Bathory might be back, he was going to stick to me like glue. Not that I minded. We'd soon have a full house once Lucius and Flavia arrived. I encouraged Aiden to call his mother, Fiona, and fill her and my best friend Christian in on the latest details. With my vampire family by my side, I felt much more confident.

While he made the phone call, I walked to the kitchen to heat up some blood for myself. After a few mugs, I grabbed a bottle of water and some Advil for Ridley. Walking into the living room, I found him slouched down on the couch about to pass out. It was still taking some time to get used to his new and improved look. Kicking him in his shin, I laughed at him. "Stay awake, party animal. I got you some water and some Advil. It'll make you feel better."

He groaned at me and sat up. "Ugh, the room is spinning. Why the hell do people drink?" he said, as he dramatically put his hand on his head.

"I was wondering if that was your first time drinking," I giggled.

"Is it that obvious?" he groaned again. Handing him the water and Advil, he popped two in his mouth and took a good slug of the water. "I'm sorry, Skyy. I should have stayed alert. It won't happen again," he assured me.

I waved off his remark with my hand. "Don't sweat it, Ridley. It's a good thing nothing major developed tonight, but from now on we should all be on our A-game. I can't believe Bathory is back," I sighed in disgust as I sat down across from him in a reclining chair.

24

Ridley kicked his new shoes off and slid his legs up on the couch. "Me either. It's like a nightmare. Can't wait to see how your grandfather flips out," he laughed.

"Not looking forward to the phone call," I said. I'd have to make the call once Aiden was done talking to Fiona. I wanted to wait and see what they had to say before calling the Divine Assassins. I *could* just portal over to the headquarters, but I didn't really want to deal with him in person. Ridley was fading fast now that he was laying down on the couch, so I went upstairs to check on Aiden.

He was just wrapping up with Fiona, and I poked his arm before he hung up. "Lemme talk to Christian," I whispered. He nodded to me, then told his mother that I wanted to talk to Christian.

Aiden handed me the phone, and I grinned when I heard my best friend's voice on the other end. "What's up, nerd?" he said, jokingly.

"Looks like you guys are coming to New Orleans," I replied.

"Yeah. You wanna come get us tomorrow? We need time to pack. And by 'we' I mean Fiona," he chuckled.

"Hey, you gotta look fashionable even while fighting the bad guys," I giggled. "Sure, just let me know when you're ready and I will portal over. Is Arabella doing well?" Arabella was a brand new vampire that had been turned after she was brutally attacked by Jack. Lucius had turned her, and she was having a hard time adjusting to her new life. Nobody really wanted to claim responsibility for her, and she was terrified of Lucius because he was rather harsh on her. None of us were fully convinced she was not a spy for Jack.

"She's doing great, but I am guessing she won't be thrilled to see Lucius again. But we can't leave her on her own, so I guess she'll be coming too," he answered.

I wasn't thrilled about having another new vampire to babysit...since I was still trying to get used to the new world myself. Having to drag her around everywhere we went, with so much temptation in this city, was going to suck. "Yeah, but I

25

think Lucius might have had a talking to by Flavia. He's a changed man these days. He might be nice to Arabella, we'll see," I said.

"Can't wait to meet Flavia. I'm thrilled for Lucius," Christian replied.

"She's awesome, you'll love her. Well, I'll let you get going. Just let me know when you want us to pick you up, and Ridley and I can portal you over here to New Orleans," I told him, as we said our goodbyes. Seeing Christian always lifted my spirits. We were both vampires now, and it was nice to have some normality in this crazy new world we were living in. He and I had been friends since high school, and though we had a little bit of a bumpy road a few months ago, our friendship has never been better.

After that phone call, I decided I should probably call my grandfather and let him know the latest developments. Dialing the number, I nervously waited for him to pick up. "Hello, Skyy," he greeted me on the other end.

"Hey Grandpa. I've got some bad news," I started out. He asked me what was wrong, and I filled him in on everything that had happened, including the good chance that Bathory was alive again.

"We always knew it was a possibility. I will get some men ready, and we will head your way as soon as we can. I'll arrange another rental house nearby for my men so they don't have to bunk with the vampires. I want as little conflict as possible," he told me. "Don't do anything drastic until we get there, Skyy," he added, knowing my knack for always getting into trouble. We chatted a little while longer, and then said our goodbyes.

Flopping down on the bed next to Aiden, who was already clicking away on his laptop for one of his many businesses he ran, I placed my hand on his chest and sighed deeply. This would probably be the calm before the storm, judging by how crazy things had been in the past with Bathory. Aiden closed his laptop, and urged me to snuggle in closer to him. Putting my head on his chest, he ran his fingers through my long hair. "I wish that we were all getting together under better terms. Or better yet, that just you and I were on our private honeymoon island instead of here hunting bad guys again," I said, yawning at the end of it.

Aiden leaned over and kissed the top of my head. "I know darling. I wish we were too. My only hope is that we can find Bathory before she becomes too powerful again. We'll let Ridley get some rest, and then get back out there tomorrow night and see what we can uncover," he assured me.

"I love you," was my reply, as I closed my eyes for a few moments of rest. His familiar scent comforted me, and soon I drifted off to a peaceful sleep. Vampires don't need to sleep every day, but it does help if we get at least a couple of hours in. As long as we keep our blood supply up, we can go days without it if we need to. But I take every chance I can get to snuggle with Aiden, and still hang on to some of my old human ways of life.

Hours later, I was woken up by my phone ringing. It was Christian letting me know they were ready to come over. He'd forced Fiona to pack light, much to her dismay. After a quick kiss from Aiden, and a mug of blood, I went downstairs to see if Ridley was up yet. He was still passed out on the couch, so I poked him with my finger. "Ridley! Wake up, we have to go get Fiona, Christian, and Arabella," I shouted.

It startled him awake, and he shot up on the couch like the house was on fire. His hair was a mess, and he had been drooling out the side of his mouth. Wiping it up and looking around confused for a moment, he finally spoke. "What time is it?"

"Time to get your drunk ass up. Let's go," I told him, as I laughed.

He glared at me angrily, and stood up. "Fine, fine. Let me use the restroom first and brush my teeth, then we can open up portals," he mumbled, as he walked off to the bathroom.

Ten minutes later we stood in the kitchen of our rental house, and conjured up our portals to France. They shimmered faintly at first, then grew in size until they were fully operational. We now had two portals in our kitchen, shimmering and glowing brightly. While you could see through them, they looked like pools of misty water when fully open. I blew Aiden a kiss, and stepped through mine. I was used to the rush of travel by now, and stepped out on the other side to see Christian and Fiona waiting for us.

Ridley emerged from his portal right after me, and Arabella joined the group shortly after our arrival. We left our portals open since we were traveling right back to our same location. I hugged Fiona and Christian, and shook Arabella's hand. I didn't know her well enough, and didn't fully trust her enough, to hug her.

"Shall we?" I gestured, pointing at the portals.

Fiona smiled at me, and said, "Go ahead and take Christian and Arabella first, then come back for me."

I reached out for Christian's hand, and he hoisted his backpack of clothes and toiletries up onto his shoulder. Holding onto him tightly, I moved us into the portal. He wasn't as used to it as I was, and it is very disorienting. We stepped out on the other side and he walked to the kitchen table to sit down after the journey. Arabella and Ridley came through next, and he turned right back around to get Fiona.

Once we were all gathered in the kitchen in New Orleans, I offered up blood to my friends. The portal takes a lot out of those who are not used to it, and all of them wanted some. We had nothing but time to kill now. We had to shut the blinds and curtains in the house, since Arabella did not have sun protection yet. The Divine Assassins didn't trust her enough to perform the spell on her, so we'd have to reassess the situation again. I could tell she was uncomfortable in the room though, and she stuck close to Fiona.

"So Arabella, how have you been? Are you finally getting used to the vampire life?" I asked her, hoping to break the ice.

She gave me a shy smile and nodded her head. Her long, wavy, chestnut brown hair was up in a high ponytail that was just messy enough to be trendy, no doubt something that Fiona told her was in style. Her makeup was perfectly done as well, and I could only imagine the two of them shopping and staying up all hours doing hair and makeup. "I'm adjusting; Fiona is a huge help. I like it in France, but I miss my family and friends. Each day gets a little easier," she replied honestly.

"Good. You're looking much better than the last time we saw you. Hopefully we can track down your old friend Jack and finish him off once and for all," I told her, trying to lift her spirits.

She just nodded and took another sip of her mug of blood. Fiona was standing next to her, flashing her perfect smile at me. As mother-in-law's go, I got pretty lucky. She was sweet, kind, and caring, and really seemed to like me. But every chance she got, Fiona wanted to get her hands on my hair, or try to do some kind of crazy make-over on me. She was very into fashion, and I was just the opposite. I like to think I get by just fine in my normal, everyday clothes, but Fi keeps telling me what a rare beauty I am, and that I should let it shine.

"So what is on the agenda for this evening?" she asked me, as she fluffed her gorgeous, wheat-blonde hair.

"We're waiting on Lucius and Flavia to let us know they are ready. They are also bringing a new friend with them, someone he met in Russia. Once they are here, we were thinking about hitting up an underground vampire club that Ridley and Skyy scouted a few nights ago," Aiden explained.

"Sounds like it'll be a blast..." Christian said, sarcastically.

I laughed, and added, "Yeah, it's pretty pathetic to see all the emo goth people in there pretending to be vampires. But even scarier how many actual vampires there are in this city preying on the humans. They are none the wiser, and think they are humans role-playing. You'll see...this place is totally weird."

"Yeah, and wait until you see the awesome pants Skyy is making me wear tonight," Ridley chimed in, and I burst out laughing even harder.

Fiona started laughing too at this point, and demanded that Ridley show everyone the pants. He huffed off to his room and put them on, and the whole kitchen erupted in laughter upon his return. Ridley stood there turning bright red and pouting. "Hey, you know I think it'll be a good idea if we all swing by the store and get clothes. You know, so we can 'blend in' better. Right, Skyy?" he said, glaring at me.

"You make a good point, Ridley. Maybe we should. We found a cool shop down in the French Quarter, maybe we'll hit it up once the sun goes down for some clothes for everyone," I said, still laughing.

And that is exactly what we ended up doing. We were still waiting on Lucius and Flavia, apparently she was having major panic issues over using the portal, and Lucius was trying to talk her into it. So while we were waiting, we hit the shop Aimee worked at. She was happy to see us, and walked over to hug Ridley and me right away.

"Hey guys! What's up!" she greeted us cheerfully.

After introducing all of our entourage, I explained to her that they were visiting and wanted to have some fun tonight with us at a goth club. She went to work right away picking out clothes for Christian and Aiden, and Fiona and Arabella dragged me off to the ladies' section to browse the racks. Ridley followed Aimee around like a lost puppy dog, and it was obvious he had taken a liking to her.

Fiona picked out a short, black leather dress, and a pair of black super high heel shoes. Arabella was advised to buy a deep red latex pair of pants, with a matching halter top that left little to the imagination, and some shiny black high heels.

It didn't take the girls long to find their outfits, and we made our way over to the men, who were protesting non-stop. I could hear "No way!" "Wouldn't be caught dead in that!" pretty much over and over from across the store before we even got to them.

I wrapped my arms around Aiden's waist from behind and asked him how it was going. He turned to me and gave me a look that said he wasn't happy. "Look Skyy, I'll wear black…but not this stuff. Can't I just get by with a black t-shirt and some black jeans?" he begged me.

"How about that and this black leather jacket?" I replied, as I took a stylish jacket off of a hanger and handed it to him. He shrugged into it, and checked himself out in the mirror.

"I can handle this, I suppose," he whined.

"Ok good...you're done. Now let's get Christian sorted out," I said, as I turned to Christian and smiled.

"No way. Not doing it," he said firmly.

Ridley piped in, "Hey, nobody is going to look sillier than me, so you guys have to do it too."

"I'll *maybe* do something like Aiden. Jeans, t-shirt, jacket. Maybe," he replied, standing his ground. He crossed his long arms over his chest for added effect.

"Fine, let's get you in a pair of jeans," I replied as I began to snatch up a few different pairs. There was another black leather jacket that was similar to the one Aiden was getting, but it had some silver studs on the wrists, so I tossed that in the pile and guided him to a dressing room.

After a lot of arguing and persuading, we finally got him into something we could all agree on. I called Lucius and told him to bring some black jeans and a black shirt as well, and he assured me he had an awesome jacket he could bring. Flavia would need something to cover her entire body, so I asked him her size, and picked her out a bright red latex cat suit similar to the one I bought, but picked out a pair of matching gloves to go over her hands as well.

Flavia had been held captive and tortured for centuries on end. Metal anchors had been placed under her skin that they would attach silver chains to, so she could not move or escape. They were magical in nature, and it took a collaboration of Divine Assassins, a Metallan Fae named Yttrium, and the vampires to get them out of her body. They covered her from below her neck, all the way down to her ankles, and the magical potions we used caused some sort of reaction under her skin. Her skin now glowed a pale white color in the locations the magical anchors used to be. All in all, we removed about thirty of them, and she struggled to keep her skin hidden when she had to be around humans.

Hopefully this latex was thick enough to cover the lights up. That settled everyone up for having something goth enough for the vampire club. We paid Aimee, and she asked where we were going tonight. Replaying the conversation I had with her cousin Pierce the other night, I was about to make up a lie so that she wouldn't ask to come, but Ridley opened his stupid mouth first.

"We found another underground club. It's pretty goth," he blurted out.

"Oh, is it The Dead Rose?" she inquired. She was from around here, and probably knew of all the hip places to be, but I didn't want to be responsible for her being around a bunch of vampires.

Once again Ridley replies, openly telling her yes. "That's the place. Been there before?" he asked.

"Oh yeah, lots of times. It's totally weird, a lot of freaks, but they play good music on Tuesdays," she said cheerfully. "Want some company?" she added.

Ridley smiled at her, and nodded. "Sure! Do you work late again tonight?" I sighed. Just what we needed. Not only would we have to watch out for Arabella tonight, but also this stupid human Ridley was drooling over.

"No, I get off at ten tonight. I can meet you guys there," she replied, clearly happy to be included in our outing.

We settled the bill, and got into our newly upgraded SUV. The car didn't cut it anymore, we needed more room. I swatted Ridley in the back of his head when we got in. "You dumb shit. The last thing we need is for a human to get caught up in this stuff with us. What if something happens to her?" I growled at him.

He put his hand to the back of his head dramatically. "Ow!" he exclaimed. Sighing, he went on, "You're probably right. I didn't think about that at the time. She said she's been there before though, so it isn't like she hasn't been exposed to vampires."

"Right, but her being around us might get her into trouble she wouldn't have gotten into on her own. Bathory AND Jack would recognize us in an instant. If you want to talk to Aimee that's fine, just don't drag her along with us to clubs where she could get killed, or worse…taken as a hostage or a victim," I shot back at him angrily.

We drove back to our rental house in relative silence, and once we arrived we had more time to kill before we could head to the club. Lucius finally called to let us know he'd talked Flavia into the portal, though she was not happy about it. Ridley and I went over to his villa in Italy right away to get them.

Flavia was indeed very nervous about the portal, but I greeted her with a huge hug. She had been through so much, and I really liked her. A tiny little thing with beautiful long red hair similar to mine, green eyes, and a feisty personality, she rounded out Lucius' rough edges perfectly. "Hi, Flavia! Great to see you. Try not to get too stressed out about the portal. It'll be fast and over before you know it," I assured her.

Lucius came over and gave me a big hug as well. It was like total opposites; he was a huge beast of a man, and Flavia was a tiny wisp of a thing. "Hello, my sweet little Skyy. This is my friend Sergei," he said, as he introduced me to his new Russian friend. Lucius had recently met up with him, and learned a lot from him about his ability to wield and control fire. In the past he'd had a few outbursts that he could not control, and they seemed to be sparked by his emotions. Sergei had taught him how to control it and use it to his advantage. The two of them would be awesome to have on our team.

Holding my hand out to Sergei, I shook his hand. "Nice to meet you, Sergei. This is my partner, and friend, Ridley Whitmore," I said, as I motioned over to Ridley. They shook hands as well, and Ridley took Sergei through the portal first then came back for Lucius. I'd take Flavia with me, since she was so scared.

Lucius had to comfort her and calm her down once more before she'd finally agree to go. It was so adorable to see my big, scary friend being so sweet and gentle with his true love. I'd never seen that side of Lucius before, and it warmed my heart.

They embraced and kissed once more, before he finally led her over to me and placed her hand in mine. "I'll see you in just the blink of an eye, Flavia. I promise it'll be alright," he said, as he grabbed onto Ridley's hand and stepped through his shimmering portal.

Flavia was visibly shaking with fear, but I grasped her hand even tighter and assured her it'd be ok. She reluctantly stepped closer to the portal with me, closing her eyes as tight as could be. I guided her closer and closer, until we finally went through it. Moments later we emerged on the other side, and Lucius ran over to her, gathering her up in his humongous arms.

To everyone's shock, Flavia was smiling. She kissed Lucius on the cheek and looked down at her body to make sure it was all still there, before announcing, "That was actually quite exhilarating!"

We all chuckled and agreed with her. "I told you it wasn't so bad!" I replied. "Once you've done it, each time will be easier!"

Fiona was dying to get over to Flavia to meet her, and Lucius made all the introductions. My vampire family was once again together, and I felt great security in that fact. Flavia told everyone her story about why her skin was glowing, and we heated up mug after mug of blood before we started to get ready for the night at the vampire club.

The girls all went into my room, and as expected, Fi took the wheel with the hair and makeup. She insisted on doing each and every one of us, and I just let her have her fun. By the time we were all done up, it looked like we were a bunch of mistresses out on the prowl for the night. But I had to admit, we looked hot as hell. If not for the damn high heeled boots, this was a pretty sexy outfit.

The men were dressed and ready to go long ago, and their eyes almost popped out of their heads when they saw us all enter the room. Aiden stood up and smiled at me, and I noticed his eyes begin to glow with arousal. He made his way across the room, and took my hands into his, then spun me around to get a better look. "Wow. You look amazing," he said, as he slapped my butt. The tight latex made a loud *"wakoosh!"* sound when his hand connected with it.

I laughed as I looked over the men. "You guys look like The Lost Boys," I told them as I took in all the jeans and leather. Lucius actually looked pretty damn cool, he had on a really long black leather trench coat and big black boots, along with some black leather gloves. He put on a pair of shades, and had his long hair back in a ponytail. His friend Sergei had on ripped black jeans, and a plain black t-shirt...but it worked. His eyes were a really unique golden color, and he had thick black hair. He matched Lucius in height, but Lucius was far more muscular.

"Let's get this show on the road," Aiden called out to everyone. Earlier that evening he went and got an additional rental car, since we would not all fit into the SUV. I piled in with the girls, and drove one of them, and the men all piled in the other one. Parking in the French Quarter sucked. We parked in one of the overpriced lots, and walked several blocks to the nightclub. Thankfully I didn't feel pain like I did when I was a human, or my feet would be killing me in these heels by now, but I did stumble many times on the uneven pavement and cobblestone.

About three blocks from the club, a group of four vampires passed us, and I immediately recognized the one from the night before that had used Bathory's name. He recognized me as well, and we locked eyes as they passed. I clinched Aiden's hand, and looked up at him. We both looked back at the vampires as we kept walking, and saw they were looking back at us as well. Shit.

Aiden knew exactly what I was thinking. I couldn't risk having any other vampire hear our conversation, so once we were outside the nightclub, I took my phone out of my purse and typed out what was going on, then passed it around to everyone so they would be informed. Aimee met us outside of the club, much to my dismay, but we got in with no issues. She came alone tonight, which was probably for the best.

Arabella was already struggling before we even got inside the club around all of the humans out and about on the streets of the French Quarter. I grabbed her hand once we were inside, and went to the bar. "Two Bloody Mary's please," I told the bartender. He was a vampire as well, and knew we wanted the real deal. Even though I had some blood before I left, I was struggling inside the club as well. There were plenty of people bloodletting in public here, and the smell was intoxicating.

Our large group procured two tables that we pushed together along the wall, and Arabella and I drank our Bloody Mary's happily. Just as we were finishing, I noticed the vampire we had passed in the street earlier walk through the door. His eyes were on me immediately. Kicking Aiden's leg under the table to get his attention, I held the vampires gaze. He was with one other vampire, and they took a table near the front of the club, positioned so that they could see our table.

Perhaps he was just curious who we were, having never seen us before last night. But, more than likely, he was somehow involved with Bathory and recognized us. Which was just what we didn't need right now. I tried to play it cool, and act as though his presence was no big deal. As the club began to get more crowded, the music got louder. It was mostly humans, with about fifteen percent being real vampires at this point. The cigarette smoke, and clove cigarette smoke was enough to make me choke, and made the club hazy.

Aimee tried to get Ridley a drink, but I gave him a look that could kill, and he got the point. Instead, he went to the bar for her and ordered her drink. He came back with a soda for himself, and a cosmopolitan for her. The vampire was looking at us every single time I glanced over to his table, and finally Aiden got pissed off enough to get up and say something.

I tried to grab him by the arm, but he shook me off, and nodded his head to Lucius who followed him over to the table. It was easy to hear their exchange, even over the blaring music. "Greetings, gentleman," he started out, in a friendly tone. "Can't help but notice you checking us out, is there something we can help you with?" Aiden said, making his point right away.

Not getting up out of his chair, the vampire who kept staring at me replied, "We saw you in the club last night, and now here tonight. You are not local. What brings you here?"

"We are new to town, just moved here a few weeks ago," was Aiden's short reply.

"Are you affiliated with one of the Coven's? What are your names?"

"I'm Mike, and this is James. We are not affiliated, or looking to be affiliated with any coven at the moment," Aiden said, lying to the vampires.

"I am Claude. Who is the red head with you?" he said as he nodded in my direction.

I could see Aiden physically tense up when he brought me into the conversation. "That is my wife, Evelyn. What is your concern with her, if I may ask?"

The vampire finally stood up, still looking my way. "Someone in my Coven might know her. Tell me, where did you move here from?"

I could tell Aiden was getting more frustrated by the minute, but he kept his composure. "California."

The vampire that was with him never spoke a word. Claude replied to Aiden with skepticism, but didn't call him out. "Very different here than in California," he said.

"Indeed. We are still getting used to things. I'm sure you've mistaken my wife for someone else, we don't run in very many vampire circles. Take care, Claude," Aiden said, as he ended the conversation whether Claude wanted to or not. Lucius followed him back to our table, and they sat down in silence.

Aiden took my hand and kissed my cheek, his way of assuring me everything would be fine. Which I knew from experience that it wouldn't be. Something was REALLY off with that vampire, if he knew Bathory, and was curious about me, things would get messy sooner or later.

The night at the club was fairly uneventful. None of the other vampires there triggered anything suspicious, and Claude stayed for quite some time, before walking out the door with a young, unsuspecting female. I wondered what was in store for her.

We insisted on giving a ride to Aimee when we left the club around four in the morning. She was going to take a cab, but with the events that had happened tonight, we didn't want to take any chances. She didn't live too far from the French Quarter, so it wasn't a big deal. Ridley and Lucius sat in the back seat with her, and I drove with Aiden in the passenger seat. Once we made sure she was safe and sound, we hauled ass back to the rental house.

"I'm sure all of you heard the exchange with Aiden and Claude. What are your thoughts?" I asked the room.

Christian was the first to speak, "I think he's connected with Bathory. It's not good if she finds out we are here this early on."

Fiona nodded in agreement. "I think so as well. There is no way that it would be a coincidence, if you said you saw him the night before talking about Bathory. She probably has everyone on the lookout for us," she said glumly.

I sighed as I plopped down on the couch and began to unzip my boots. "Of all the damn places she could have landed, why did it have to be here? Or why did it have to be at all? I thought we were on the hunt for Jack, and here we are once again faced with both of them!" I exclaimed in anger, as I threw one of my boots across the room.

"Yes, but look on the bright side, if she has been brought back to life, she will be very weak. So maybe it is a good thing we found her this quickly," Ridley said, trying to lift my spirits.

"Maybe, or maybe not. None of us have ever dealt with these phylacteries before now. Let's hope for the best, and until we get a lead, there isn't much we can do but keep going out on the streets looking for clues," I finished.

The room dispersed after that, and we all went to our separate bedrooms. Aiden prepared me a warm mug of blood, which I sipped slowly, enjoying every moment of it. I was stressed out beyond belief, and he knew it without me even having to say a word. "Your grandfather should be here soon, and we will come up with a plan, Skyy. I will admit, it makes me very uneasy being in this city of so many vampires," Aiden confessed, as he sat down on the bed next to me.

Sipping my blood, I nodded to him. "I agree. Jack will be working alone, as always. But who knows how many vampires Bathory may have had in hiding, or how many she could have recruited since our last meeting. And let's not forget the dark fae who are on her side. The sheer number of vampires walking the streets here with nothing to hide is shocking," I commented.

"I will admit; this is probably the largest concentration of vampires in one small area that I have ever seen. The culture here is perfect for them to prey on humans," he told me.

"Ugh. I hope Grandpa brings plenty of toys to play with, we are going to need all the help we can get from the Divine Assassins. I'm also going to insist on Flavia and Arabella getting the sun protection spell as soon as he arrives. We can't risk anything right now."

I finished my mug of blood, and all I wanted to do was get out of this stupid latex cat suit and relax in Aiden's embrace. He unzipped me as I climbed out of it and went to the bathroom to wash my face. Moments later we were snuggled up in the warm bed in one another's arms. I could hear Fiona and Christian humping like rabbits, and Lucius and Flavia going at it as well. Ridley and Arabella were talking in the living room. Sometimes I really just wanted to tune all of the world out…one of the downsides to being a vampire I guess.

The sun was about to rise, and I finally heard Arabella head to her room. Aiden and I snuggled in silence the entire time, and finally he kissed my forehead and told me, "Today is a new day. We will figure things out, Skyy. We always do."

# Chapter 3

Claude walked into the mansion that the small gathering of vampires were residing in with Elizabeth Bathory. His new friend Anton was right behind him, with the young woman from the nightclub in tow. They had both had a taste, of course, but she was meant for Bathory. She perked up at the sound of her two minions coming up the stairs with a human.

It took a lot of effort for her frail body to do anything in her weakened state. She only recently was able to stand up without the help of Claude. The young, attractive woman was in her early twenties, and she had perfect skin. Her blood smelled wonderful, and was calling out to Elizabeth like a siren singing her song to a ship of sailors in the ocean.

The girl was under mind control, and smiled at Elizabeth in greeting. "Hello," the girl said cheerfully.

Elizabeth sat up in her bed, returning the smile. Her long, black hair was a tangled mess that she tried to brush out with her fingers for a moment, before she tossed it behind her back. "Hello, child. Come and sit with me." The smile was not meant to be friendly, but it was instead a smile of knowing that she would soon be relishing the girl's blood.

She began by nipping at the girl's wrists, and drinking up the blood that flowed from there, cherishing every single drop. With each mouthful that she drank, she could feel tiny bits of strength flow through her body. It was a long, and painful road to recovery, but she was not one to quit.

Patience, however, was never one of her strong suits. The nipping and drinking would only satisfy her for a moment or two. She wanted more, as always. "Claude. Get the bath ready," she barked out at her servant. She was grateful for his service, for he was the one to resurrect her, but he was nothing more than a minion in her eyes...weak and powerless, but he served a purpose.

Claude nodded silently as he went to the bathtub they had fashioned in her bedroom suite. The tub was caked with old, dried blood from the countless girls before this one. He pulled on a thick chain, and a metal device he had rigged with hooks descended down from the ceiling. Anton went over to Elizabeth, and lifted her weakened body out of the bed as if she were a child, and carried her naked form over to the tub. He placed her down in it gently, and she shooed him away with the flick of her hand.

Elizabeth had given strict orders to each of her "sleeper vampires" that she had hidden across the world with her phylacteries to build her a home in a remote area with no other houses around. She would not be bothered by people asking questions when the screams eventually came from the house. Claude had obeyed her orders to a tee, and built her mansion decades ago in the woods.

Elizabeth squealed in delight when Claude lowered the hooks down. "Get in the tub, and face me," she told the girl. The young woman did as she asked, without hesitation. She was still being mind controlled…for now. The hooks were hanging just above her head now, but she didn't pay any attention to them, and continued to smile at Elizabeth.

"Now, take your clothes off. Quickly!" she demanded. Once again the young, beautiful woman did as she was asked.

The girl was now standing completely naked in front of Elizabeth, who gave a slight nod to Claude. "Lay down on top of me," she barked out to the girl. Sighing happily as she felt the warmth of the girl's body on top of her, she inhaled her scent like a wild, crazed animal. Claude moved over to the side of the tub, lowering the hooks down even more.

Overall there were eight hooks on the metal rig. He would keep the girl mind controlled until the first one was through her skin. He pinched a good amount of the skin on her back, and shoved the rusted hook through it, hearing a nice "*pop*" sound as it pierced through the flesh. The girl didn't even flinch at the pain, and Elizabeth was writhing in delight as she smelled the fresh blood from the wound.

"Now, let her mind go, Claude," she ordered. He nodded at his master, and freed the girl of the mind control. The moment it was gone, the girl screamed out in agonizing pain, which made Elizabeth grin even bigger. The girl's eyes were wide with fear and pain now, as she looked down at the woman she was laying on top of.

"What is going on?! Who are you?!" she screamed out in terror. Elizabeth grabbed her face with one hand, squeezing it tightly so that her cheeks were being smooshed in. Her nails dug into her skin, causing blood to drip down onto her bare chest.

"I am Elizabeth Bathory, and you're about to die," was her macabre reply.

Claude was manhandling the girl with ease, as he continued to puncture the hooks into the skin and muscle on her back. The blood was dripping down her sides and gathering on Elizabeth's body, warming her up even more in the spots it touched. She reached down with her fingers to soak some of it up, and licked it off of her fingers one by one, savoring the taste, as she became stronger and stronger.

The final hook was in place, and the girl was panting and convulsing from the pain. Her eyes were rolling in the back of her head, as she went in and out of consciousness. The more she struggled and screamed, the more Elizabeth liked it.

"Alright, Claude. Lift her up!" she commanded.

"No! Please, no! No! No!" the young woman screamed as Claude yanked on the huge chain that would raise her up. The pain of her body weight pulling on the hooks was more than she could bear. The blood was dripping down freely now from the wounds, splashing all around the porcelain tub.

Elizabeth was sliding her hands around in the blood, and smiling with her eyes closed as the girl managed to get out a few loud screams. The metal sound of the chains clanging from her body convulsions was like music to her ears. A slow fountain of blood was pouring over her shoulder blade, and Elizabeth opened her mouth greedily to allow it flow into it.

Her body was now covered in blood, and she rubbed it into her skin like it was lotion. But it wasn't enough. The girl eventually passed out and stopped resisting and screaming, which made her mad. It wasn't any fun anymore, and she just wanted to get to the end result at this point. "Claude, finish her off," she said, anticipating what was coming next.

Claude nodded silently, and went over to a small table full of tools he kept. Knives, saws, razors…plenty of things to cut and torture with. He never knew what Elizabeth would be in the mood for, and learned from experience it was better to be prepared than to make her upset.

He walked over to the limp body with a huge knife in his hands. It had serrated edges on the blade, to saw through the muscle and cartilage of the throat. With one fast motion, he sliced a deep wound across the victim's neck. Quickly moving out of the way, so as to not upset Elizabeth, he walked back over to the table to clean the knife off as he watched his master enjoy the final course.

She lifted her head up to the sky, and smiled as the blood poured freely down onto her from the gaping wound. She gulped it down ravenously, and soon her hair was soaked in blood. What wasn't going in her mouth or hair, Elizabeth rubbed into her skin. Her body would absorb it through her pores, and she could feel the energy flowing through her for the time being. It wouldn't last long, but with each victim she got a little bit more of her strength and magic back.

The last few drops were trickling out of the girl's neck and Elizabeth let out a sigh of happiness. She hated when it came to the end, but knew that Claude and Anton would bring her another tomorrow night. Until then she would sleep through the wretched daylight hours, content with her bloodbath.

She always wanted to sit in the tub for a while after her bath, and wanted the lifeless body to hang there until she got out. Looking at the corpses always made her feel better. She sucked the youth, life, and beauty right out of them. She'd be beautiful again one day as well, but it would take many, many more victims.

As Claude was about to leave her alone for a while, he walked over to the tub. "There is one more thing I think might make you happy tonight," he said, as he reached into his back pocket to get his phone. He pulled up the picture that he had taken earlier of the group of people he followed into The Dead Rose. Holding it up for Elizabeth to see, he waited for her response.

She shot up from resting against the back of the tub and snatched the phone from his hands. Examining it closely, her eyes shrunk down to slits. Confirming once and for all that it was indeed Skyy and her vampires, she slowly sank back down against the back of the tub with a huge smile on her face.

Claude took his phone back and silently walked out of the suite. He could hear Elizabeth laughing manically for over twenty minutes. She was too excited to sit and admire her kill after seeing the photo. Skyy Huntington was in New Orleans. It was almost too good to be true! Everything was working out, and it seemed as though she wouldn't have to travel very far once she was back to full strength to get revenge on the Divine Assassins.

While she still had the energy, and before all of the blood dried up completely, Elizabeth would perform the ritual that would seal the young woman's soul into a writ in her new book of souls that she was recreating. It would take many years to get back what the Divine Assassins took from her when they destroyed her old book, but she was determined.

Elizabeth harvested a large chunk of skin from the girls back, and stretched it over a board to start the process of tanning it to use as a page in the new book for later. Claude would finish the process, as she would soon become too weak to continue. Going over to a large trunk, she carefully removed her new book of souls, carrying it like it was the most precious thing in the world. Placing it on a table, she went back to the trunk and removed one of the already tanned pieces of skin from a former victim.

Performing the ritual would suck all of the energy out of her that she had just gained from her bloodbath, but it was all worth it. She went over to the bathtub, and gathered up some of the blood in a small cup. There was already a spot on the floor that she had designated with a ring of blood to do the rituals. She used the fresh blood to ignite the magic in the area, and watched as it burst to life. Tiny sparks of blood magic began to sparkle within the circle, and Elizabeth smiled.

She dipped a special tool into the cup of blood, and began to scribe her black magic spell down on the piece of skin. The blood lit up as she wrote and chanted the spell, glowing a soft red color on the skin. Blood magic particles were flying all around Elizabeth like a tiny tornado now, illuminating the area with their brightness. A loud 'sigh' came from the corpse in the bathtub, and Elizabeth smiled when she heard it. The victim's soul was now bound to her book, tainted with her black magic to do her bidding, and to give her power whenever she called on it.

The blood on the skin eventually stopped glowing, meaning the spell had succeeded and her work was done. The room darkened as the magical circle slowly died down, and Elizabeth stood up with her book grasped tightly in her hands. She placed it back in the trunk, and quickly went back to her bed before nearly collapsing. After sleeping for several hours, she planned on instructing Claude and her vampires to ramp up the abduction of victims. She wanted at least three or four a day from now on.

She would also tell them to become more aggressive with persuading the local covens in New Orleans to align with her. There were many of them, and so far two covens had taken her side. Something odd was going on between these covens, and truthfully, Elizabeth had never seen this many vampires in one city before. Usually, one coven ruled over a city, two at most. Here, there were over a dozen of them…that she had discovered so far. And most of them had deep rooted issues with the other ones. They would get over their petty differences and join up with her, if they knew what was good for them, she thought to herself.

Elizabeth drifted off to sleep, with the rotting, soulless corpse still in the room with her. Tomorrow she would send her vampires out to find out more about Skyy, but for now it was imperative that they did not discover her location in her weakened state. Perhaps she would need the protection of her Dark Fae….

# Chapter 4

Grandpa had called a few hours ago letting us know that he and his men were coming in this afternoon. They rented a house on the same street we were on, and I think both the Divine Assassins, and the vampires alike were happy about not having to share living quarters with one another. No matter how much we worked together, there would always be tension from the Divine Assassins towards the vampires, which made the vampires uneasy and afraid they might get pissed off enough to silver one of them or even worse, kill one of them.

I wasn't exempt from any of it just because I was Killian Huntington's granddaughter either. I was a vampire now, so a good chunk of the Divine Assassins didn't really trust me either. They tolerated me at best, but I got shady looks all the time. You'd think they would know that ALL of the vampires in my circle were here to help by now. We've risked our lives a dozen times already to prove it.

Nonetheless, I was happy to see my grandpa, and gave him a big hug when I went over to their rental to see them. Aiden, of course, was by my side, and greeted him warmly as well. The men were still portaling back and forth from headquarters to the rental house with supplies, gear, and magical gizmos. He got right to the point immediately after our greeting. "Has anything new developed since we spoke?"

Shaking my head, I sat down on a very uncomfortable chair in the living room to get out of the way of all the Divine Assassins moving around the house. Aiden followed my lead and plopped down on a couch. "So far, no. We still have no lead on Jack, and as I mentioned on the phone, we are almost positive Bathory is here as well."

Grandpa sighed angrily as he ran his hands through his snow-white hair. "Well, I have one group of men I assigned to hunting for Jack. They will be out and about at night, since we know he can't be out in the daylight. Any tips you can give them that you have already uncovered would be great. The rest of us will begin focusing on finding Bathory," he explained.

Nodding my head at him, I added in, "We have already discovered that there is a huge, and I mean *huge*, community of vampires here. Several covens, which according to Lucius and Aiden, is very strange. And they all seem to be at war with one another. We saw a heated exchange in a nightclub that escalated very quickly. The bar owner defused the situation, and he seems to know a lot about what is going on around here. I would like the chance to try to get him to warm up to me some more."

"We need all the information we can get. If these vampires are all fighting amongst themselves, that may be an advantage for us if Bathory is trying to recruit them to her cause," he said as he began to dig around in a bag looking for something. "Ah-ha, here we go. I brought some books for you to read. It is everything we could find about phylacteries, and how they work."

Taking the stack of books into my arms, I cautiously approached the next subject. "I know this is a sensitive subject, Grandpa, but putting the sun protection spell on Flavia and Arabella would be really useful to us right now."

He sighed, and I think he knew I wouldn't stop pressing him until he finally gave in. "Fine, fine. I suppose you are right. At the very least, I like Flavia and I trust her. I am still not sure about the new one though. Let me go back to the base, I will make you a learning potion that will teach you the ritual for the spell, alright? We'll perform it with your help this time."

Not expecting that much from him, I grinned at him and thanked him over and over. "That sounds great, Grandpa!"

He opened a portal shortly after that, and went to the base, and I stuck around the rental with Aiden who was sitting on the couch the whole time working on his laptop. Leaving him to his work, I offered to help organize the items the men were bringing in. One of the few Divine Assassins who didn't have an issue with me was there. Keith and I had worked together in London, where his partner, Logan, had been murdered by Jack. He was a good guy, and I was happy to see him again.

"Keith! Glad to see they put you on the team here!" I told him happily as I shook his hand.

He smiled back at me warmly, "Hello, Skyy! Good to see you as well. I thought we were done with Bathory, but looks like round two is coming up, huh?"

Rolling my eyes in disgust, I replied. "I know, I thought so too. This should be interesting. Look forward to working with you on it though!"

Before we could say much more, Grandpa portaled back in to the rental house, and took me aside. He handed me a small vial with a potion in it. The liquid was clear, and looked like water, but it had a slight glow to it. "As soon as you drink this, we can head over to your rental and perform the sun protection ritual on Flavia and Arabella," he said, as he called out to a few of his men to join us.

I popped the top off of the potion and chugged it down. It had no taste at all, and I hoped that there would be no side effects. After my eyes turned purple and started swirling, and then after Flavia's skin began to glow, I wondered if there was some sort of conflict with this magic and vampires. My entire body started to feel warm all over, but it faded within seconds, and I shrugged it off and went to find Aiden.

"We're going back to our place to do the sun ritual on Flavia and Arabella," I told him. He nodded, gathered up his stuff, and took my hand.

The walk back to our house was very quick. Grandpa, Keith, and five other Divine Assassins were right behind us, and we called out to the girls as soon as we entered the house. They were overjoyed that they would finally have the sun protection as well. For someone like Flavia, who had been a vampire even longer than Lucius, this would be the first time she could safely go out in the sun in centuries.

The Divine Assassins and I all stood in a circle and took one another's hands. We began the spell, and I could feel the energy flowing through us. My body was almost buzzing with it, and I could feel my skin warm up again as the spell was near completion. The sun shield was now on both of the women, and they thanked us over and over for it.

The Divine Assassins and Grandpa all left to get back to moving into the rental house, and I needed to get together with Ridley. He was probably still asleep after the late night out, so I climbed the stairs and knocked on his door. After some grumbling on the other side of the door, he opened it up and moved aside so I could enter.

"We need to get together with that guy Pierce. Aimee is his cousin, so do you think you could talk her into setting up a meeting with him sometime today?" I began, wasting no time.

He was still half asleep, with a wrinkled t-shirt on, and ruffled up hair. Rubbing one of his eyes, he replied "Sure, I can give her a call and see." After that he just stood there staring at me.

"Well? Do it then," I laughed, waiting for him to call her.

"Oh, now you mean?"

"Yes, now would be great," I chuckled again.

Ridley navigated back to his bed, and grabbed his phone off the table next to it. He pushed a button and waited as the phone dialed Aimee. It rang for a long time, then went to her voicemail. As he was leaving a message, she called him back. "Hey, Aimee, it's Ridley," he said. I rolled my eyes. As if she wouldn't know who it was.

Apparently she was on the same page as me, and replied back to him cheerfully, "I know it's you, silly!" I could see Ridley blushing from across the room.

"I won't keep you long, but wanted to know if you might have a way for us to get in contact with your cousin from the club?"

She sounded shocked at the request. "Pierce you mean? Uhh, sure. But why, what's up?"

Ridley sighed out loud, and I could tell he didn't know what to say. "He was telling us some information about a few things the other night, but he was really busy and we never got to finish talking. Just wanted to ask him a couple of things." I was impressed with his comeback; he usually wasn't that good at lying.

"Oh, okay. He doesn't open up the club until night time, so he might still be asleep, but I can call him and see. Let me call you right back." They hung up, and a few minutes passed before she called him back. He picked up right away. "He said you guys can meet him up at the club at five if you want. He'll be there restocking," she informed him.

"That sounds great, thank you so much Aimee," he said sincerely.

"No problem. What are you doing after that?" she asked.

"I'm not sure yet," he replied as he looked over at me. I shook my head no at him. We weren't going to have time for him to be out on a date tonight. The safer we kept Aimee, the better.

She sounded disappointed on the other end of the phone, but Ridley told her he would call her if he planned on staying out after the meeting with her cousin. "Ridley, I can tell that you like Aimee, as more than a friend, but we have our hands full here. Her cousin would kill us if anything happened to her...literally. She has no idea that vampires exist, and we should probably keep it that way," I told him as nice as I could.

He stood up, and smiled at me, pretending that it didn't bother him. But I could tell that it did. "No biggie, Skyy. I agree with you, and I don't want to see anything bad happen to Aimee because of me. Let me hop in the shower and we can head over to the club to meet Pierce at five."

Closing his bedroom door behind me as I left, I made my way back to the bedroom I shared with Aiden for some blood. Deciding it might be a while before I would get another chance to drink, I packed a small cooler full in case I needed it while I was out and about. Aiden came in and started to change his clothes. "When are we leaving?" he asked me as he threw his shoes into the closet.

"As soon as Ridley is ready. He just woke up, and is taking a quick shower," was my reply, as I helped him take his shirt off. I saw Aiden's eyes ignite as he looked down at me and smiled. Placing my hands on the waistline of his jeans made them glow even more.

"We have at least a half hour then, right?" he grinned at me. Nodding my head, I stood on my tip toes to kiss him, as I undid the buttons on his jeans. He stepped out of them, and lifted me up as I wrapped my legs around his waist. Carrying me over to the bed, I lifted my shirt up and threw it onto the floor as he sat me down on the comforter. We scooted back onto the bed, and he wasted no time in undoing my bra…something that he quickly became an expert at, considering I was his first, and only, sexual partner in all of his centuries on earth. His warm breath felt amazing as he pulled one of my nipples into his mouth, gently scraping it with one of his fangs. He knew that drove me crazy. Aiden's hand toyed with my other nipple as he twirled the one in his mouth around his tongue. Before long, my panties were soaked, and he reached his hand down from the nipple, to between my legs.

Softly sliding my panties aside, he inserted one of his fingers inside me, as he caressed my clitoris with his thumb. Moaning out in pleasure, I pulled his face off of my breast and kissed him deeply. Using my other free hand, I wiggled out of my panties and guided Aiden inside of me. As much as I loved his foreplay, I knew we were short on time, and it had been over twenty-four hours since we had last made love.

Wrapping my legs around him, he pumped me slowly at first, then faster and faster. I bit into his neck the more excited that I got, and licked up the blood that dripped from the wound. I knew that excited him, and he fucked me even harder as I moaned out in pleasure. I came first, and he was not far behind me. Aiden stayed inside me for another few minutes, as I continued to lap up the blood from his neck gently.

Hearing that Ridley was just about ready from the other room, Aiden reluctantly rolled off of me, and kissed my cheek. Smiling back at him, I softly kissed his beautiful lips once more before we had to get dressed. I glanced in the mirror as I picked up my clothes, and my eyes were glowing like two purple neon signs in the night. I'd need to put my contacts in before we headed out into the city.

I quickly washed my face and ran a brush through my hair, popped in my magical contacts that Ridley made for me, before Aiden and I met him downstairs. Fiona and Christian were just coming back home, and asked if we needed any company.

"Sure. We are going over to a club that Aimee's cousin owns. He knows a lot about the vampires here, and I am hoping to get him to answer some of our questions. It'll be dark soon, so I wouldn't mind the extra backup," I explained.

The five of us packed into the SUV and headed back into the congested French Quarter for the evening. There was a bouncer outside the club when we arrived, even though they didn't open until midnight. Apparently he knew that Pierce was expecting us, and let us in without saying a word. The place looked totally different in the daytime with the lights on. The swank, dark façade it had at night quickly transformed into a run-down building by day. The seats on the cushions were mostly patched up, there were sticky spots all over the floor. You could see all the places that careless patrons had scribbled on the wall, and all of the places the paint was peeling off.

Pierce was over at the larger of the clubs many bars, cleaning glasses. He didn't look thrilled to see us, as expected. I was shocked he even agreed to it in the first place, but was glad that he did. "Three vampires with you this time?" he noticed.

I smiled at him to greet him, and extended my hand out to shake his. He dried his hand off on the towel and shook it, as well as Aiden's. "Thank you for meeting us, Pierce. These vampires are part of our family. This is Christian, and Fiona," I explained, pointing to each of them as I introduced them.

"You refer to your coven as your *family*, is it not a coven?" he questioned.

Fiona spoke up before I could, turning on her fantastically perfect smile. "No, we are not a coven. Each of us are together by choice, and can leave at any time. We all live separate lives most of the year. Skyy was in need of some help, so we came out to New Orleans to aid her."

We watched Pierce's face as he took all of the information in. I could tell this was something he was not used to hearing. "So, you are not led by one coven leader?"

Fiona shook her head, her beautiful blonde hair swinging around her shoulders as she did so. "No, we don't need a leader, because we are all family."

"And what kind of trouble is Skyy in? I knew that it was too good to be true. I don't like seeing that Aimee is caught up in any of this," he grumbled.

Aiden was rubbing my back softly, and I took the opportunity to take the lead back from Fiona. "Well, one of the reasons I wanted to meet up with you, is that you seem to have some insight on the different covens here in New Orleans. You mentioned Bathory, and we have a long history with her," I started out.

"I've lived in New Orleans my whole life. Been running this club for fifteen years, and the vampires have made it quite difficult over the years. I've never met any vampires quite like you folks though," he admitted.

"That is why none of us have any desire to be part of a coven," Aiden chimed in.

Pierce nodded his head. We could tell that he was still on the fence about deciding if we were legit or not. "I have never had any of the vampires, or coven leaders for that matter, come to me like you folks are. The ones here have no respect for humans at all, or for our businesses that we run. There are several vampire-owned and operated bars and nightclubs in the area, and they want to drive us humans out of the ones that we run."

"You mentioned they were all at war with one another. Can you give me any details about that?" I prodded.

He sighed loudly. "I dated a vampire once, when I first opened the club up. I had no idea what she was until we were already a year into the relationship. I never questioned it because

I ran a business at night, and slept all day as well. She was the daughter of one of the coven leaders here, and was murdered by the daughter of another coven leader. This has been going on for decades here. I have no clue how it all started, but they kill each other off like flies. Now that Bathory is back in town, some of them are taking up with her cause, and they are being forced to get along."

"So, you can definitely confirm that Bathory is indeed here, in New Orleans?" I questioned.

"Far as I know, from what I have heard the bloodsuckers talking about, yes. No offense, you guys seem like decent vamps and all. Like I told you the other night, you guys should pack up and leave before shit really hits the fan here," he replied. "So what kind of trouble are you in?"

"You wouldn't believe us even if we told you, but let's just say that Bathory and I have a long history. We actually thought we had killed her a few months back. But apparently she has been resurrected, and our biggest fears have come true. She *has* to be stopped, before she gains all of her strength back," I told him.

"Wow...well that sounds serious. I know all about her, from my deceased vampire girlfriend I mentioned before. If you guys are here to put a stop to Bathory, count me in for any help. I'll keep my ears and eyes open for any kind of information that might help."

"We really appreciate it. But that isn't all. I hope you're ready for this one. You know Jack the Ripper? The serial killer from the 1800s?" I started out.

Pierce nodded his head yes, and I continued. "Welllll, he kind of isn't dead. Bathory turned him back in the 1800s, and they had some kind of twisted love/hate relationship. He has never stopped killing, and we chased him out of London and followed him here to New Orleans. So we are here to try to stop him as well," I chuckled. As if the story couldn't get any weirder, right?

54

"Shit. You really do have your hands full. What does he look like? I have seen the news with all those crazy murders lately. So he only goes after women?"

"As far as we have seen, yes he only goes after women. The problem with him is he is VERY solitary. He works alone, has no friends, and looks very normal. The last we saw him, which wasn't too long ago, he had chestnut brown hair that was just above his shoulders, but he usually ties it back. He also has a moustache and goatee, isn't very tall, but he is very muscular."

"I'll keep my eyes out for people fitting that description." He slid a piece of paper across the bar and handed me a pen. "Write your number down, and I will be in touch if I see anything weird."

I jotted my number, and Aiden's number, down on the paper and slid it back to him. "What other places around here would be good for people watching? We are just hanging around trying to listen in on conversations to possibly get some clues," I asked.

Pierce gave us a few places that the vampires frequented, and told us a couple of places to avoid. "The covens here are nasty for the most part. You don't want to cross them, and it's best to just steer clear of the vampire-run places."

"Got it. Trust me, we don't want to be here either," I told him.

As we were about to leave, Pierce asked us, "Hey, how come you guys are out in the daytime? Just dawned on me. Never seen a vamp out in the sunlight."

"Another long story. We've got ties to an Order that can perform magic. The organization formed specifically to hunt, and kill Bathory. Being able to walk in the sun is one of the perks," I said, flashing him a smile. He nodded, and smiled back.

We thanked him for all of his help, and left his club feeling like it was a win. The sun would set in about a half hour, so we decided to walk around the French Quarter for a while until it was dark. The more that we walked around in the sunlight, the weirder I began to feel. Before long I felt like I was burning up with a fever, and almost passed out.

Aiden grabbed me as my knees buckled. "Skyy! Are you alright?!" he exclaimed, panic filling his voice. A group of college kids walked by and laughed at me, one of them saying I couldn't hold my liquor. At this point, I could only wish that I was drunk. I had no idea what was going on. He ushered me to the curb and we sat down on the sidewalk, Fiona, Christian, and Ridley all circled around me with concerned looks on their faces.

I put my head into my hands, and took deep breaths. Aiden quickly reached into my cooler and got me some blood. My friends blocked the view of any passersby so I could drink it down. The sun was almost totally set now, and as I looked down at my hands, I noticed that the tips of my fingers, and my fingernails, were illuminated with a soft, golden glow.

Aiden saw it too, and I locked eyes with him. "Jesus Christ. I bet you this is from that potion I drank earlier," I said. Once the sun was fully set, my skin began to cool off, and I felt much better. My fingers were still illuminated though, and we figured it would be best to head back to the car until I felt better.

"Perhaps the potion removed some of your sun protection shield?" Christian offered up as a suggestion.

"I am wondering that very same thing, Christian."

Aiden spoke up, "If your sun protection had worn off, you would have known it immediately. Without serious protection from the sun, you wouldn't have made it to the car to leave for the club without feeling like your skin was about to ignite."

"Right, but what if the spell was still active, just not working as intended?" Christian chimed in.

"We will have to perform it again tonight," was Ridley's answer.

"But, how do you explain this!?" I exclaimed as I held my hands up.

He frowned, disappointed that he didn't know the answer. "I don't know, Skyy. But we will see if we can figure it out. We have plenty of Divine Assassins that will be out in the city tonight on the lookout, I think we should get you back home and see if we can shield you again."

"I think that is a great idea," Aiden responded. Christian and Aiden left to go get the car to pick me up, not wanting me to exert myself. They were back in almost no time at all, and we drove right to the Divine Assassins makeshift headquarters.

# Chapter 5

There was no other explanation any of them could find in the database, or in any books, for what was happening to my hands. The best we could come up with, was that performing the ritual earlier that day on the others, somehow messed with my own shielding. They let me take a cool bath, even though I was already cooled down for the most part, before they performed the entire ritual on me again.

As before, I could feel my body being surrounded by warm, comforting light. We'd see in the morning if it worked or not. I wasn't going to let this stop me from being on the streets tonight, even though everyone objected to it. Standing my ground, I drank some blood, put on some new clothes, put some gloves on my hands, and we hit the road.

The French Quarter was even more packed than usual tonight, since it was a Friday. Everyone but Arabella and Fiona, who stayed behind with Arabella, was with me as we made our way to one of the smaller clubs that Pierce had told us about. Once again, we found a disgusting display of humans pretending to be vampires, and vampires openly feeding in public on other humans. The music was blaring, and hearts were pumping fast on the dancefloor. Unsure if it was because of the ordeal earlier or not, I was having a hard time controlling my thirst.

I pulled Aiden over to me, and whispered to him "Can you please get me a drink?" Nodding at me, he went to the bar and got a plastic cup, which they charged him for, reached into his backpack, and poured the contents of a blood pack into the cup discreetly. He handed the cup to me and I kissed him on the cheek. Aiden sat back down, and I perched myself in his lap as I sipped on the blood. It wasn't warmed up, but it served its purpose. My eyes were scanning the crowd for familiar faces, and my ears were open to all of the conversations. Nothing exciting happened for quite some time, until a small group of vampires walked in.

Three males, and two females were in the group, and they almost instantly locked their eyes on us. I tapped Aiden's leg to alert him, and the rest of the group followed his lead. One of the females began to dig around in her purse before producing a phone. They talked amongst themselves, before finally walking farther into the club. As the female with the phone walked by me, she took my picture! "Hey!" I yelled out to her as I shot up off of Aiden's lap. She quickly moved through the crowd, towards the ladies' room.

I chased her and her group through the crowd, with my vampires and Ridley right behind me trying to keep up. Amazed by her boldness, I was bound to catch her and grill her on it. Thinking that she lost me, I saw her and the other female dart into the bathroom. Busting through the door like a madwoman, I almost took it off of its hinges. She was just about to close the door to a stall when I grabbed her by her arm. The moment that I made contact with her skin, she screamed out in pain, falling to the floor grasping her arm.

Flavia had entered the ladies' room behind me, while the men stood outside. The two of us watched in horror as the vampire's arm turned black like ash. It continued to spread all over her body, until she was nothing but a pile of clothing and ashes on the bathroom floor. Her friend tried to escape the bathroom, and thank God we were the only ones in there. "Grab her!" I shouted out at Flavia, who was on it in an instant. "You guys need to get in here right now, and block the bathroom off!" I said to the men, who I knew could hear me through the door over the music.

The men, with the exception of Sergei who stood guard outside the door, were in the bathroom like a shot. Christian's mouth dropped open when he saw the pile of ash. "What the....?" was all he could manage to get out.

"My thoughts exactly, Christian," I said, in just as much shock as he was. Lucius took over restraining the female vampire from Flavia, and before long I could hear the three men she was with outside arguing with Sergei. Soon they all bust through the door, and after seeing their friend laying on the floor the fists started flying. They were outnumbered, and even though

I was still a young vampire myself, I could tell that my vampires were much older than they were, and wouldn't stand a chance.

Aiden had neutralized one of them in an instant, having pinned him to the floor with a silver dagger. Lucius was taking care of another one, as Flavia took over restraining the female once more. The third male had made a phone call, and that was not good. We had no idea who might be on the way for backup. Sergei blocked him from leaving the bathroom by grabbing him with one arm, and igniting his other hand into flames. The vampire quickly got the message, and stopped trying to fight back.

The female Flavia was restraining was hysterically crying, and for good reason. I had just killed her friend right in front of her. "Pick her belongings up," Lucius told Christian, who followed orders without questioning, since he was the closest to the pile of ash. He grabbed her purse, the phone she took the picture with, her skimpy clothing, and her shoes. Lucius walked over to the ash, and began to kick it into a grate in the tiled floor in the event a toilet overflowed. This enraged the vampire being subdued by Sergei, but he quickly shut up as he moved his flaming hand towards him.

"We need to get out of here, right now," Aiden remarked seriously.

"We cannot leave the silvered one here, he has to come with us, or we kill him now," was Lucius' reply.

"No! We'll go with you willingly, don't kill him!" screamed out the female.

"Shut up!" hissed out the vampire with Sergei. "We will not go with you!"

Sergei gave a nonchalant shrug, and with his heavily-accented Russian voice told him "Do you prefer to be burned, or disintegrated like your friend here then?" It cracked me up actually, and I laughed out loud. Everyone turned to me in shock, as I diverted my eyes to the ground and kept laughing. But before anyone had a chance to reply, the door burst open once more, and lo and behold...the vampire Claude from the night before entered the bathroom, with four more vampires.

Things were really crowded in here now. Claude recognized me instantly as his eyes darted around the room, assessing the situation. "What happened to Misha?" he asked, to no one in particular.

Nobody said a word.

He yelled out at the top of his lungs, "WHAT HAPPENED TO MISHA!" as we all jumped a little.

"I killed the fucking bitch, and if you don't shut your mouth, I'll do the same to you!" I shouted back at him. I was enraged at the whole situation by now. With no idea what was happening to me, or how I just killed a vampire by simply touching her, I was ready to rumble. "Why was she taking pictures of me?" I yelled out to him.

"Because the whole vampire community is looking for you right now. You have no idea who you've just messed with," he laughed sinisterly.

"Oh yes, I am pretty sure I do. Tell your boss hello from me, and let her know I'll be killing her again soon," I said, with venom in my voice. That caught his attention, as he clearly thought he had the upper hand here. "She didn't tell you who I was, or why you should be looking for me? I KILLED her, and I will kill her again. Don't be stupid enough to take her side, Claude," I told him.

"The only people who will be dying tonight are you and your friends. Misha was my wife for over four hundred years!" he said as he sobbed and yelled at the same time.

"Well if it is any consolation, I didn't mean to kill her," I said, truthfully.

"It isn't a joke!" he screamed out at me, his eyes were lit on fire with rage now. "Maybe I will take your love away from you!" he shouted as he darted towards Aiden. Before he was even halfway there, Sergei directed his fire in a line towards Claude, who managed to dodge the flames by an inch at most.

Lucius, who was still learning to control his fire abilities, lit his hands up as well as the brawl began. Knowing that all I needed to do was get close enough to one of them to touch them,

I looked for opportunities to get into the mix. Sergei had lit the vampire he was restraining on fire, and Lucius followed suit to one of the vampires that Claude had come in with. The bathroom was getting hotter by the minute, and the smoke was burning my eyes.

Shooting into the crowd, I placed my hand on one of the other vampires, who yelled out in agony as I watched the same thing happen to him as it did to Misha. His wrist where I touched him turned black, and his body collapsed into ashes shortly afterwards. Ridley, being a human still was having a hard time breathing in the bathroom, and I was afraid that he could suffer permanent damage from the smoke inhalation.

We were down to just Claude, the hysterical female, and one other vampire now. I shot over to the other male and touched him. He turned into a pile of ash. Claude, knowing he was defeated, ripped the door to the bathroom off of the wall and fled, leaving behind the female vampire. The bathroom was engulfed in flames, and we knew we had to get out of here as soon as possible as well. "Fuck it! Ridley, open a portal, let's get out of here that way. Nobody will be able to see past these flames!" He nodded at me, and we both began to open up portals.

Grabbing Flavia first, he jumped through his portal, as I grabbed Aiden and jumped through mine. We dropped them off at our rental house, and instantly went back for the others. The whole thing only took a matter of minutes, and we even managed to get the hostage out with us.

Fiona and Arabella came flying down the stairs with the first portal that was opened. They could see something was wrong immediately. Once we were all gathered in the living room of the rental house, I explained to the women what had happened. Fiona came over and hugged me immediately, even after I told her I was turning vampires into ash. After taking all of the other vampires through the portal, with the exception of the hostage which Ridley took, I realized that I had not killed any of them with my touch.

Ridley could see from the look on my face exactly what I was thinking, as Fiona broke off her embrace with me. "Skyy, I think this is definitely tied to that potion you drank earlier. I don't think you lost your sun shielding. I think you're *absorbing* the sunlight. It is the only thing that makes sense! Your fingers are glowing, and it happened after you were out in the sun, after drinking that potion. None of our vampire friends are affected by it, yet you're turning other ones into ash," he said, rubbing his chin as he thought more and more about it.

Flavia stood by my side, and put her arm around me as well. "Skyy, some very odd things have happened to both of us when we have come in contact with the magic and potions from the Divine Assassins. I owe them my life, but I glow like a lantern now. I think that there is something that does not mix well with our vampire blood and the magic," she theorized.

"I think you are right. It was odd when my eyes turned purple, but I have taken dozens of potions and have had no other side effects until now. I wonder if there is a common ingredient in the mixtures that could be causing these things to happen," I said as I looked to Ridley for answers.

He shrugged at me. "I don't know, but I will certainly find out," he told me as he opened a portal and stepped through it, heading to the Divine Assassins headquarters no doubt.

Lucius wasted no time in interrogating the terrified vampire hostage we had before us. "You're going to talk, or you'll turn into ash just like your friends, do you understand me?" he boomed out to the girl. I saw Arabella jump as he yelled at the girl, and I could tell that she was still terrified of him.

The female vampire just nodded at him, knowing that he wasn't playing around. "Are you in a coven with that vampire from tonight, Claude?" She nodded. "Are you working for, or with, Elizabeth Bathory?" he asked. She nodded. "Can you confirm that she is indeed here, in New Orleans?" She nodded.

Aiden came to my side, and took my hand into his, kissing the back of it for reassurance. Fiona left the room and made me a mug of heated blood, sensing that I was in need of it. I had the best vampire family on the planet.

"How long has Bathory been here, in New Orleans?" he continued with his questioning. The girl was trembling in terror;

Lucius was definitely the one who could get results out of people.

"A few weeks, I think? My father is our Coven leader, and Misha was his daughter," she sobbed. Well shit, I killed her sister. Whoops. "If you let me go, I can explain it was all an accident. I mean...it was, right? An accident?" she asked, grasping at straws.

"You and your coven have no idea what you are getting into with Bathory. What is your name?" I said, before Lucius could answer.

"Lara," was all she replied with.

"I personally killed Bathory, not very long ago. She is in a weakened state, and is trying to gain an army of vampires to help fight her battles for her, it looks like. We're going to kill her again, and you better pick the right side," I told her, as threatening as I could sound.

She seemed even more terrified of me, than of Lucius, after seeing her sister get disintegrated before her eyes. "I don't have any say in which side I get to be a part of. My father makes those decisions."

"Would your father be willing to meet with us, then?" Lucius asked her, while glaring down at her.

"After killing his daughter, and other Coven members, I doubt he would meet with you," she scoffed, getting brave suddenly.

"You just said you would tell him it was an accident," I retorted. "The only way you're walking out of here alive, is if you agree to help us."

Her eyes widened with panic when I confirmed her fear. "Our Coven has been greatly weakened in recent years. We have a bloody history with two of the other covens here, and murders take place on almost a monthly basis. He thinks joining up with Elizabeth will be our only chance at prospering once more. It is very unlikely he would listen to reason, even if it meant he would lose his only remaining heir," she said, sadly.

"Take it from me, we have plenty of experience with Bathory. She will use your father's coven for her own gain, will kill or expend any of your members, and not even blink an eye. She has no value for anyone, or anything except herself. It won't end well for your coven," I replied to her, with sincerity.

Lara began to cry again. All of us could tell she was between a rock and a hard place. "With Misha gone, you will have my father, and Claude out for blood now. They are probably declaring war on your coven as we speak. It seems like all we do here in New Orleans is kill one another. Claude has been an ally of Bathory's for many centuries, when he met Misha and joined our coven, it pretty much bound our fate with hers."

"So, you lied to us? Knowing there would be nothing you could do even if you did tell them it was an accident?" Lucius growled at her.

Still sobbing, she looked down at her hands and just nodded. Lucius walked behind her, and looked over at Aiden and me. None of us wanted to kill her necessarily, but we couldn't just set her free either. She could be lying for all we knew, and the company she kept certainly wasn't good. What Lucius did next shocked me. He silently moved his finger across his throat, meaning he wanted to kill her.

Furrowing my brow at him in confusion, I saw Aiden nod in agreement with him! Taking his hand in mine, I pulled him out of the room, and Lucius followed. We darted off of the property and out of ear range. "Are you saying what I think you're saying, Lucius? We want to kill her?" I gasped.

"Yes, we should kill her. She lied to us, and her coven is deeply rooted with Bathory. Even if we let her go, her father would never agree to a truce with us after we killed not only his daughter, but several members of his coven. Just kill her, and move on," he said matter-of-factly.

Aiden was nodding in agreement. "I agree with Lucius, milady. If we set her free, she could give away important details to her coven, and more importantly, to Bathory. She knows our location, and will tell them about your new special powers. We need to keep some element of surprise if we mean to kill Bathory."

Sighing out loud, I knew they were both right. I wish that we had just killed her in the brawl back at the club. This seemed so much worse to me than killing someone in self-defense. Though, I knew they had a point, she would probably rat us out, and we'd end up killing her again at a later point. "You're right. Both of you are right."

"I will take care of it right away," Lucius said without a second thought. We darted back to the house, and Lara sat up straight as an arrow when she saw us enter the room again.

Before he took her, I asked one last question. "Why are all of these covens here fighting all the time?"

"Part of it is territorial, too many covens encroached on already claimed areas. They would not merge covens, and began fighting over territory. Then, key members started secret relationships with sworn enemy covens, so they started murdering each other to get revenge. Smaller covens looking to get bigger, made pacts with voodoo tribes in the area, and started messing with magic they had no idea about, which caused a lot of issues. So many different things at play, that people forgot why they hated each other, and just fight to fight these days," she said glumly.

Lucius grabbed her by her arm and hoisted her up off of the chair she was sitting in, and she started protesting. "Wait! Let me at least *try* to talk to my father! Please!" she pleaded.

"You can thank Bathory for your situation. You said yourself that there was nothing that could be done. We can't keep you here, and we won't set you free. As we tried to explain, getting involved with her benefits nobody but Bathory," I explained to her. Lucius dragged her out of the house kicking and screaming. That was the last I heard from Lara, and I knew that we were already in deep shit from killing the other coven members along with her. Lucius never told us where he took her, or how he killed her, and nobody asked. We thanked him for cleaning up the mess for us, and he just nodded and smiled in return.

Ridley came back shortly after Lara had been taken away, and was smiling. "I have some good news! I think I found a common ingredient in our potions that may be causing the odd reactions." He stopped talking when he saw my face. "What's wrong, Skyy?"

"Lucius just took Lara off to kill her. She would not cooperate with us. We are already in deep here, and don't have a clue where to find Bathory. I need to talk to Grandpa. Lara told us some disturbing things, and I need to find out what he might know about voodoo," I replied.

"He is at the rental house right now, we can go over there and have a chat," he told me.

"Sure. But first things first, what did you find out about the potions?" I inquired.

"Right! Okay, so one common ingredient in all three of the potions that you ingested, and that were used on Flavia to remove her anchors, were petals or oil from the Asteraceae family of flowers. The potion you drank that turned your eyes purple had Echinacea, and purple Zinnia petals in it. Part of the magical solution we made for Flavia contained dandelion, and the sun protection spell potion you just drank had sunflower oil in it. Most importantly, it also contained Chlorophyll...which is what I think is enabling you to absorb sunlight. The flowers and sunflower oil are all from the same family, and there may be some sort of interaction when introduced to vampires," he explained.

I knew all about the alchemy ingredients he rambled off, from drinking a learning potion to help me excel at the craft faster. "Interesting. I wonder if it is something that will fade over time, or if I will keep the ability to absorb sunlight. I am going to test it out again tomorrow in the daytime. For now, let's get over to the rental and talk to Grandpa."

Ridley gathered his things up again, but gave me some advice. "Skyy, I would be careful until we know how this will interact with your body. I wouldn't want you to absorb so much that you burn yourself up," he warned.

The rest of the vampires in the house dispersed as we left for the Divine Assassins rental house. Aiden came with us, and kept his eyes and ears open along the way. We had pissed off at least one coven that we knew of already, so we had to keep on our toes. Grandpa took us into his makeshift office so we could talk in privacy. "You look worried, Skyy. What is it, my dear?" he said, with a look of concern on his face.

"We might be in huge trouble already. There was a big fight in the club last night, and we killed several vampires, including the daughters of a coven leader. Bathory is confirmed to be here in town, though we don't know where. And I apparently can absorb sunlight," I blurted out quickly.

His eyebrows perked up at my last statement. "Absorbing sunlight? How?"

I held my hands up, and showed him my glowing fingertips. "No idea. Ridley thinks it may be from Chlorophyll in the sun protection potion." I saw Ridley nod, then go into detail about the chemistry of it all.

"Very interesting. It is true that all the potions contained the petals or oil from the Asteraceae family. We must be careful with you Skyy. None of this has ever happened before, and now both you and Flavia have had odd reactions. It is one thing to have purple eyes, but absorbing sunlight as a vampire is quite scary," he said.

"I agree, it is scary, but also quite useful. If I can get near Bathory all I have to do is touch her, and she is done for. And, if I can somehow charge myself up, perhaps I can control it, or project it out from me, instead of having to rely on physical touch!" I exclaimed, feeling excited at the possibilities.

"Just be careful, please. It will be best if we discontinue potions for you until we can dig deeper into the side effects, and how they interact with vampires. Perhaps we should draw some blood."

"That is probably for the best. While this is pretty darn cool, I don't know what other kinds of reactions I might have to future potions, and some of them might not be so great. But the real reason I am here, is something that one of the vampires we dealt with mentioned. She said that local covens were forming alliances with voodoo tribes. What do you know about voodoo magic?"

"Depending on the person, or persons performing it, voodoo can be very similar to some of the things we practice here within the Divine Assassins. Protection spells, healing spells, things like that. Voodoo uses a lot of physical items, such as charms, gris-gris, or dolls. But in the wrong hands it can do plenty of harm. It is not unheard of for vampires to seek out voodoo practitioners to help them rid themselves of their enemies, or protect their covens from them," Grandpa explained.

"Do we have any books on the subject back at headquarters I could pick up?"

"Sure. If you want to portal over there, we could do some bloodwork and grab some books," he said.

"Aiden, if you want to meet me back over at our house, I can portal in directly to there. We shouldn't be too long," I told my husband.

"As you wish. Please be careful," he said as he kissed my cheek and left the house.

We opened up two portals, Ridley and I went together in one, and Grandpa in the other one. Headquarters always depressed me. It was underground and there were no windows, so it was always dark. Most of it was concrete which made it even more depressing. The fact that the Divine Assassins were comprised of almost all men, made it a complete bore-fest in the decoration department. Grandpa pulled two books from the vast library, and handed them to me, and then he drew some quick blood in the lab. I was back at my own rental house in no time.

Aiden and I sat down to talk almost as soon as we got back. "Skyy, I don't like the idea of you having this sun power. I think that your grandfather and Ridley are right, you should remain out of the sunlight, since nobody knows what might happen."

"I know it worries you, Aiden. But this might be a HUGE game changer for us. There is nothing I can do about it now; the damage is done. I'd like to at least see if I can become more powerful in the sun or not."

"You are right, but please promise me that if you start to feel odd like you did yesterday you will come back inside immediately? If you want to test it out, do it here at the house so you can come back inside quickly. Please?" he begged me.

"I promise. Grandpa is right though; I shouldn't ingest anything else until they can do some research. We need to focus on finding Bathory quickly though, before she can recruit anymore of these local covens. This is a huge mess, and I hope that we aren't too late," I sighed as I sat on Aiden's lap and wrapped my arms around him.

I killed time until sunrise reading the books on voodoo, and about the phylacteries. It seemed like no matter how many times we might kill Bathory, as long as she had a phylactery to gather her soul in, she could be resurrected. There was one loophole though: if she was killed in another dimension, say…The Gloom…her soul would not be captured. As if it wasn't hard enough to kill her here, now I had to devise a plan to get her into another dimension to kill her.

Grandpa was right about voodoo; it did seem very similar to some of the things the Divine Assassins practiced. I gathered as much information as I could from the books, and placed a bookmark inside them for later reading. The sun was up now, and I wanted to do my experiment.

Knowing full well that it could kill me, I decided the risk was worth it. Aiden was a nervous wreck, but knew that I was going to do it with or without his permission. Fiona and Christian came outside with us as well, and they were as equally worried as Aiden was.

"Well, here goes nothing," I said, as I stepped out onto the grass in the backyard. A few minutes passed, and then I started feeling warm like I did yesterday. It quickly progressed into feeling like I was in an oven, and I began to get weak. Aiden rushed to my side as I let my knees collapse into the grass. "Hang on, Aiden. Let me see how much I can handle," I told him, pushing his helping hand away for the moment.

"Skyy, this is ridiculous! You're going to get yourself killed!" he exclaimed, then gasped out loud. The others gasped with him.

I looked up at them with a confused expression on my face. "What?! What's wrong?" I asked.

Aiden didn't give me time to answer, he scooped me up out of the grass and ran inside with me. Fiona and Christian were right behind us, and slammed the door to the patio. Fiona and Aiden were placing their hands all over my skin to feel if I was warm.

"Your eyes, Skyy. Go look in the mirror," Christian said. He was clearly shocked by something, which scared me.

My body was slowly cooling off now that I was inside away from the direct sunlight. I took a few deep breaths, and stood up. Aiden was already on the phone calling Ridley and my grandfather to come over immediately. I looked in the mirror, and gasped.

My eyes were now illuminated just like my fingertips were. The purple was nowhere to be found. They were glowing like two tiny suns.

"Wow," was all I could manage to get out.

# Chapter 6

Ridley and my grandpa were there in a flash, and they did the same thing everyone else did when they saw me. They gasped. Both of them rushed over to me, and began inspecting me, placing their hands on my skin, and getting a closer look at my hands and eyes.

"Your hands are illuminated much more than they were yesterday, Skyy. And your eyes...I don't even know what to say," Ridley said, astonished.

"I feel fine now that I have cooled off!" I explained. "I want to go back out there."

Every single person in the room shouted "No!" at the same time.

"I want to know what will happen. If I can use this to our advantage, and kill vampires from a distance, it is worth it!" I exclaimed, defending myself.

"It isn't an option right now, Skyy. You are not going back out in the sun. At least not today," Aiden said, firmly. I sighed, as I took a mug of blood that Fiona had made for me out of her hands. "I won't see my wife burn up alive in front of my eyes."

Flavia, Lucius, and Sergei had all joined in when they heard what was going on in the kitchen. My grandfather had some interesting news to report on the blood we drew at the headquarters yesterday. "When we inspected it under a microscope, your blood cells are illuminated...just like your hands and eyes. I am literally at a loss for words, Skyy."

"Well, that's comforting," I said, sarcastically. Nobody knew what was going on with me. Even though I thought this could be the most powerful weapon any of us could wield, it was also something dangerous that could probably kill me. "Okay, I will stay out of the sun for the next few days, and see what happens. In the meantime, what do we want to do about tonight?

Claude and his Coven will be scouring the streets looking for us after what happened last night."

Lucius spoke up. "Indeed, they will be. I am uncomfortable not knowing how many they might have with them."

We all agreed with that statement. I sipped on my mug of blood while the group tossed around ideas. "Don't forget, we also have teams of Divine Assassins out in the city looking for Jack, and signs of Bathory as well. The covens won't suspect them, or be looking for them. We can use our men to hopefully plan a surprise attack. I will tell them to be on alert for Claude. My suggestion is that he needs to go, and very soon," Grandpa chimed in.

"There is no argument from me. He is very dangerous, and now he has a reason to get revenge on us," Aiden replied. I was thrilled to see Grandpa actually being civil, and almost kind, to my vampires. Baby steps.

"I think that your group of vampires should lay low, and let my Divine Assassins out in the field do some reconnaissance work tonight. There could be an ambush, or larger numbers gathered in hopes of catching you guys out in public tonight," he suggested to us. While none of us liked to sit around while there were two dangerous vampires to find, I knew what he said was the best plan.

"It isn't ideal, but it is the best thing for now," I agreed with him.

"We don't want to be caught off-guard, or walk into a trap. Have your men stay in constant contact with us through the night, Killian. We will be ready to attack at a moment's notice," Lucius told him. Grandpa nodded, and then left to give his orders to the Divine Assassins.

Since I was stuck indoors for the rest of the day, I decided to get back to reading, while Aiden clicked away on his laptop next to me in our bed. As I turned the pages, I began to notice something odd. Each time the friction of my fingertips hit the corner of the page to turn it, my fingertip would feel warm. I started to snap the pages between my fingers to test it out more, and sure enough it would warm up each time.

Placing the book next to me on the bed, I moved on to snapping my fingers quickly. The result was shocking! I could see tiny tendrils of illuminated mist exploding between my fingertips! "Aiden! Look!" I exclaimed. He watched me do it several more times, each time faster than the other, as more and more of the bright mist flowed out of my fingers.

Aiden didn't know what to say, and I could tell from the look on his face that he was uncomfortable with what was happening to me. But he didn't say anything, he just set his laptop aside and watched me snap my fingers. Soon, I was snapping so fast that it was just constant friction between my fingertips, and before long I had an actual ball of the illuminated mist forming from my hands.

It was taking shape, and I could manipulate it as it floated above the palm of my hands. It was soon the size of a softball, and growing as the moments passed. I stopped the friction, and watched in awe as the ball of mist hovered before me. Moving my hands back and forth, I was able to control it and move it wherever I placed my hands!

"Aiden...this is incredible. This is like concentrated sunlight!"

"I know, Skyy. I can feel the heat emanating from it from over here." Aiden replied, as he looked at the mist in amazement.

"Well, what do I do with it? It isn't shrinking now that I have stopped the friction with my fingers," I said, wondering what to do next.

"I have no idea. This is very dangerous; I think we should move this out of the house before something bad happens. Which means you need to go outside in the sun again. Quickly this time, Skyy," Aiden said, as we both jumped up off our bed, and moved towards the door.

Rushing towards the back door that led outside, we picked up Christian and Lucius along the way, who were curious what was going on. "Whoa!" was all Christian could get out, as he followed hot on my heels.

Aiden opened the door and I stepped back out into the sunlight with my ball of mist. I had no idea how to detach it from my hands, even though it was floating above them, it was moving along with me as if it were attached with an invisible string.

I already started to feel the effects of the sunlight, just being out here for the brief moment. I didn't want to pass out with this thing in my hands, so I flicked my wrist outwards toward the yard, and watched the ball of mist shoot out from my hands towards a huge tree. The glowing ball of mist shot towards it with lightning speed, and when it collided, it exploded in an eye-blinding burst of light.

We all put our hands up to our eyes, and wondered if we were permanently blinded. At least three minutes passed before any of us could see, but Christian was the first to get his eyesight back. I heard him say, "Holy shit, Skyy!" and knew that it couldn't be good.

A few moments later I got my vision back, and saw the tree. Well, what was left of the tree, that is. It had turned into a pile of glowing ash and embers. Christian acted quickly, and ran to get the water hose to put out the fire before it could spread. Aiden and Lucius just stood there staring at it in disbelief. The sun was kicking in even more now, and I felt weak and hot.

"Get me inside please, I feel like I am going to faint, Aiden," I called out weakly to him. He was so distracted with the tree burning up, that he almost forgot about me being in the sun. We were back inside in no time, and I started cooling off almost immediately. I looked down at my hands, and realized they were illuminated even more than earlier in the day. "How do my eyes look? It seems every time I go out in the sunlight, I get more of a 'charge' and absorb more of its power."

"Your eyes do seem brighter," Lucius remarked.

"I guess this answers the question of if I can control it, and project it," I chuckled, as Aiden handed me some warmed up blood to regain my energy.

75

"We don't fully understand this yet. It is just as mysterious as Sergei and I being able to control fire, but there must be ways you can control your new power. Though this is not something I imagine you're thrilled about having to live with, I think this will turn the tide of our battle. We can control fire, and sunlight! Our enemies won't even have to come near us; we can burn them alive from a distance, Skyy!" Lucius exclaimed, in a rare showing of excitement.

Smiling back at him and his enthusiasm, I nodded my head. "You're absolutely right, Lucius. Now, we just need to find them."

# Chapter 7

Elizabeth Bathory was constantly being startled awake by her minion, Claude, howling in agony over the loss of his wife, Misha. She was frustrated beyond belief, and could care less about the useless wife, or her sister and the other coven members that had been incinerated. All she wanted was to sleep, and regain her strength for the girl that he would bring her tonight.

"Claude! Quit your miserable howling!" she bellowed out for the fifth time that hour.

Having had enough of her telling him to be quiet, he stormed into her living quarters, uninvited no less! How dare he?! "They KILLED Misha! Are you not even remotely concerned about the fact that the one you are looking for can kill vampires with the touch of her hand?! We have to retaliate, we have to gather our allies and attack them tonight!" Claude demanded, waving his hands around like a madman.

"The only person who is going to be attacked tonight is you, Claude, if you don't leave me be to get my rest. We will deal with Skyy when the time comes, but for now we won't act in anger. You make stupid mistakes when you act out of anger," Bathory replied to him from her huge bed. She was naked, and still covered in dried blood from her last victim.

Claude was frantic, and pacing the room. He didn't get the not-so-subtle hint to get out of her living quarters. "I have been an unquestioning, faithful servant to you for centuries, Elizabeth. Please! Please help me avenge my Misha. I have never asked anything of you until now," he pleaded.

"Claude, do you think I like laying in this bed, day after day, weak and frail? The girls you are bringing me are helping me get stronger, but I cannot *do* anything to help you right now. If you and your coven act alone, without my help, you will get yourselves killed. I need you to continue with the plans we made. Keep recruiting the local covens, or break them apart to recruit members for all I care. We have lived for centuries, we just have to be patient," Bathory explained to him.

"How is she able to turn vampires to ash by touching them!?" he exclaimed.

"I have no idea, but we will find out. Our vampires must be instructed not to attack Skyy, or her allies, until we know more. I know it is difficult for you, but you must observe her, and watch her. Don't engage her!" she ordered.

"I will do as you ask, Elizabeth."

"Can you please ask Valentina to come up to my chambers before you leave for the night?" she asked him.

Claude nodded, regained his composure, and closed the doors behind him as he left. There was no point in arguing with Elizabeth. He would get nowhere with it. But he damn sure wasn't going to sit around for who knows how long waiting for her to get her strength back. Skyy and her friends would die at his hands long before that. She would be none the wiser. Most of the vampires living in her secluded mansion were loyal to him. And he had remained loyal to her, up until now.

She wanted her dark fae captain up in her chambers, which meant he had to go up into the attic where the fae mostly kept to themselves. He was disgusted by the dark fae, and avoided them as much as possible. He knocked on the door at the top of the small set of stairs that led to the attic, and one of the lower ranking fae opened it for him. His dark skin, and piercing red eyes emerged from the blackness of the attic. "Yes?" he said, as he looked at Claude.

"Elizabeth wishes to see Valentina," was all Claude said. The dark fae nodded at him before closing the door, and Claude went about his business. They would go out and observe, as she ordered. But they would act much sooner than she thought.

Bathory drifted back off to sleep while she waited on Valentina to arrive. The one-armed captain softly knocked on the door to her chambers, and was given permission to enter. She bowed and greeted Bathory, as much as it killed her. The dark fae race and Bathory had a very strained relationship. They agreed to work together, only out of mutual benefits from one other. But the dark fae quickly became fed up as Bathory abducted and experimented on their own kind, trying to take on the powers of their race. She would also drink from them, and kill them by the dozens, which angered their leader.

For the moment, the dark fae were still instructed to provide Bathory with protection and knowledge.

So, Valentina put on the best fake smile that she could, and asked how Bathory was doing today. "Better each day, Valentina. I can feel myself getting stronger with each new soul I take."

Internally, Valentina rolled her eyes, but on the outside she just nodded her head and smiled once more. "Glad to hear it. What may I assist you with today?" she asked, wasting no time getting to the point.

"I need you to summon Rex for me. There are some troubling developments with my situation, and I would like to ask him a few questions," she replied, not even bothering to lift herself up in the bed to speak to Valentina.

"Very well, I shall return with him shortly," the dark fae replied, as she left the living quarters. She opened a portal to her home world of The Gloom, and stepped through it. Breathing in the thick air, she smiled. Having to live in Bathory's dimension was draining, but she suffered through it. Opening up her wings, she took flight into the ever-twilight skies towards the Royal Tree. Rex was the Prince of the dark fae, and regarded with the highest esteem among her race.

She spotted the Royal Tree in the distance, the largest tree in The Gloom. It towered over all other trees, and was luxurious on both the inside and the out. The Royal family, and all of the top ranking dark fae lived within. The guards let her inside without hesitation, for she was high among the ranks herself. When she was able to reside in The Gloom, she called the Royal Tree home as well.

She flew with haste to Rex's quarters. There wasn't a dark fae female alive that didn't have a crush on him. He had it all: looks, personality, he excelled at dark magic, and he was humble and down to earth. Valentina got excited each time she was able to be around him. After gently knocking on his door, he called out for her to enter.

His quarters were decorated in dark blues. Midnight blue velvet curtains hung over the large, stained-glass windows that were crafted eons ago into the Royal Tree. The black ceiling sparkled with magic that looked like stars in a night sky. His round bed was huge, and had dark blue satin sheets on it, that she would die to spend one night with him between. Her eyes found Rex right away.

He flashed her a killer smile, and lifted up off the ground to flutter over to her. His massive, feathery wings were three different colors, showing off his Royal lineage. Any non-Royal dark fae only displayed one color in their wings. But Rex's were crimson red, midnight blue, and the glowing edges were a deep plum shade. They were a sight to behold. He tucked them back behind him as he landed.

He rarely ever wore a shirt, and Valentina didn't mind that at all. His arms and back were tattooed, and they were illuminated with magic that glowed brightly. His perfectly sculpted muscles in his arms and abs were begging to be caressed. His gorgeous, deep blue eyes sparkled as he looked at her. It was all she could do to spit out a greeting to him. "Hello, Prince Rex."

He laughed at her. "Valentina, how many times must I tell you to just call me plain old Rex? We have been friends since we were children. There is no need for the formalities," he reminded her kindly.

Valentina's cheeks, though her skin was quite dark, blushed in embarrassment. "Yes, Rex. As you wish."

"What brings you here today?" he asked, as he went over to a small refreshment table to pour some honeyed wine. He extended a goblet out to her, and she gladly accepted.

Sipping on the honeyed wine before answering, she informed him that Bathory wished to see him. He rolled his eyes. "Ugh. What does she want this time? I am so sick of that hag," Rex stated.

"There is some kind of issue, she didn't elaborate. No doubt she needs your magical assistance," Valentina explained.

"No doubt. That is all she ever wants. That and my blood, and my body." Valentina cringed internally when he mentioned that. "My father has been discussing ways to break this alliance we have with her. And I have been pressing him to put someone else on in your place, so you can be home where you belong, instead of next to that snake," he told her, which shocked Valentina. That he cared about her well-being touched her deeply.

She bowed to him, humbled. "Thank you, Rex. Your kindness is unheard of."

He flashed that smile at her once more, which made her knees weak, and then finished off the last of his wine. Shrugging on a plain black t-shirt, he sighed out loud. "Well, best get it over with. Let's go." Rex said as he gestured towards the portal he had opened back to Bathory's dimension.

Valentina stepped through it first, and instantly felt the life being sucked out of her as she entered back into Bathory's mansion. If Rex was right, she would only have to suffer through this for a little while longer. She escorted Rex up to the room that Bathory was in, and excused herself back to the attic. Wrapping her wings around herself, she kneeled down in the darkness of the attic, and daydreamed of Rex.

Bathory welcomed the handsome dark fae known as Rex into her quarters. He was always a sight for sore eyes. Rex was truly a beautiful creature, and she relished in his presence every chance she could get. He acted as though he equally enjoyed her company, and she was none the wiser. She pat the bed next to her, and gestured for him to sit down.

Immediately, she began to touch him, caressing her fingertip along his magical tattoos. It made his skin want to crawl, but he just smiled down at her instead of showing his disgust. Before Skyy had killed her, Bathory was actually quite attractive. But it didn't make up for all the ugly things she did to both humans, and the dark fae alike. Now she was just a shriveled up shell of her former self. "May I?" Bathory said, as she gestured to Rex's wrist.

He knew she wanted to bite him, and drink from him. She always did. He offered her his wrist, and turned his head the other way. It disgusted him to watch her drink blood, like some crazed predator. And it was beyond beneath him to agree to it, but for now he did as his father instructed him to do. He felt the prick of her vampire fangs pierce his skin, and then heard her slurping up the blood.

Elizabeth loved nothing more than drinking from Rex. His blood flowed with magical energy that made her feel alive again. She quivered with excitement as she gulped down his sanguine fluid. The scars on her back where she once would sprout her own version of dark fae wings began to tingle, and this is what excited her the most. Something about his blood ignited the magic left behind from before she was killed. For a short while, she almost thought that the wings would form again. But they never did. Once she was back to herself, she would resume her magical experiments of mixing her DNA with the dark fae.

His blood did more for her than thirty human girls did. For a short while, she felt almost as good as new. Being in the presence of this divine, handsome, being made her wild. She moved from his wrist and softly nipped at his arm all the way up to his neck. Elizabeth's body was visibly shaking now with the anticipation of more blood.

Straddling Rex's lap, she tore into his jugular vein, taking in his magical blood once more. Smiling as she watched it drip down onto his shimmery, inky skin, Elizabeth's breathing began to pick up pace. She caressed his over-sized manhood through his pants as she drank. Even though he wasn't thrilled about her drinking from him, he was still a man after all, who had a naked lady sitting on him rubbing his cock. The only part about this exchange he could consider tolerable was the sex. And it was mediocre at best.

"Take your pants off," she demanded. It killed him to have to let her talk to him this way. *Nobody* in The Gloom would dare boss him around. But he did as she asked, and took his pants off. She immediately slid down onto his fully erect penis, and began to gyrate as she continued to drink from his neck. He closed his eyes and imagined a beautiful, sexy, dark fae instead of the hag. Elizabeth proceeded to slide up and down his cock, faster and faster as she drank, until she climaxed. He followed suit shortly after.

Panting and exhausted, she leaned back to look at him. Her skin was radiant, and her dull, brittle hair looked shiny for the time being. She tried to kiss him, with her blood soaked mouth, but Rex turned his head away. "You know I don't like that, Elizabeth." he warned her.

She scoffed, climbed off of his still-erect penis, and flopped down onto the bed on her back. She didn't like being told no, but would tolerate it coming from Rex. It was worth it.

Wasting no time at all, he asked her what she had summoned him here for. "Right to the point, eh Rex? What can you tell me about someone having the ability to turn a vampire to ash, just by touching them?"

Rex was intrigued by this question, as it was something he had never heard of before. "Hmm. I have no idea at all. Was it another vampire that did this, or a human?" he inquired, wanting to know more.

"Another vampire. Who is also part of The Order of the Divine Assassins that I told you about."

"The magic they use is something I have little to no knowledge about. I can feel the energies in the earth if they preform it while I am in this dimension, but it is rare. It sounds like they have developed some sort of spell," he theorized.

Elizabeth was running her fingers through her long hair as she continued to relax on her back. "I may need some serious help from your people soon. Things are escalating here very quickly. Quicker than I am recovering. We can't let her get any stronger."

"Who is it?"

"The one who killed me," she growled.

Rex didn't have all the answers, but he knew one thing: he needed to find the vampire who killed her, and he needed to form a secret alliance with her. It didn't matter that her, and her group of friends, had slaughtered his people in cold blood.

"I see."

"Can you ask your Elder fae if they might have any knowledge of this kind of magic? She can decimate my vampires with a single touch. Perhaps they know how to counter it," Bathory asked him.

"Yes, I will inquire. I must take my leave now, but I will be in touch if I find anything out," he said, using the excuse of wanting to get on the case right away to make his exit. He could not wait to be away from her. Grabbing his pants off the floor, he stepped into them and ran his hands through his short hair to make sure he looked presentable.

He left without another word, and went to the attic to find Valentina. She was sitting in a corner, with her wings wrapped around her tiny body. "Valentina," he whispered to her, as he touched her shoulder. Hearing his voice made her smile. She figured he would leave without saying goodbye. But she could smell the blood and sex on him, and it quickly killed her mood.

"Yes, Rex?" she replied.

He held his hand out to her, and she took it. There were roughly sixty other dark fae in the dark attic, all in their tiny light-forms, hovering around the room. It was barely enough light to see in, but dark fae had excellent vision, and he could see Valentina looking up at him longingly. He knew she had a deep crush on him, and he somewhat returned the feelings. But his father would never, ever let him be with one of the captains of the dark fae Guard. "Come with me back to The Gloom. We have much to discuss," he told her.

She smiled at him, and they stepped through the portal back to The Gloom hand-in-hand. The first order of business was to bathe in the springs behind the Royal Tree to get this stench off of his body. Then Rex would tell her all about the plan he was slowly, but surely, piecing together to rid themselves of Bathory once and for all.

# Chapter 8

Jackson Ripleigh had been in New Orleans for several weeks now. He was finally getting used to the ins and outs of how the city worked, and was settling in. He quickly discovered that there were several groups of vampires and covens all living in the area. Being a man of solitude, this did not sit well with him. He had been approached twice already about talking to Coven leaders, which he of course declined.

Finding victims was easier than ever, and he had no issues feeding, or finding women to satisfy his twisted pleasure. In the few weeks he had been in town, he had already killed seven women. He was sitting in a bar on Bourbon Street flirting with his eighth victim now. A pretty, young college girl from Iowa here with her friend, he noticed right away that she was promiscuous from the way she was dressed. The fact that he had bought her several shots of tequila just amplified it. She was here alone, her friend was back in the hotel room hungover from last night, but she refused to stay in and be bored. That would be the biggest mistake of her life.

Dawn was flirting with Jackson like crazy once he suggested that they move to a smaller table, instead of sitting at the crowded bar. She scooted her chair closer to him without him even having to ask. He didn't have to use any kind of mind persuasion on this one, she was his for the taking. Jack was putting on a great act for her, smiling, and gently playing with her long blonde hair. He'd caress his pointer finger along her neck as he did so every now and then.

He worked on Dawn for over four hours, before asking her if she'd like to go back to his "hotel" with him. She didn't need any convincing, and gladly accepted. He helped her up out of her seat, and waited patiently as she excused herself to the restroom before they left the bar. Dawn needed a lot of help walking, and standing up straight, and Jack was happy to oblige.

Guiding her down some side streets to his designated spot that he would kill her in, he was abruptly stopped by six vampires. They instantly took over her mind, and demanded that she come over to them. Jack grabbed her by the wrist, and yanked Dawn back to his side. "Excuse me, sirs! This is my blood for the night!" he told them, shocked at their rudeness.

"No…it isn't. We've been keeping tabs on you, and the leaders have decided that your killings stop tonight. We don't know who you are, or where you came from, but killing people in public like you do is a good way to get us all exposed, or worse…killed. So, whatever sick fetish you have, you need to start cleaning up after yourself, and doing it somewhere private," said one of the vampires.

They commanded Dawn to come back over to them once more, and she obeyed them without question. Jack's amber eyes were glowing with anger now, as he contemplated what to do next. With six of them, there was no way he could engage in a fight and come out alive. He'd lost this battle, but would be damned if he would do as they said.

"At least let me feed from her," he begged. He didn't put in all that hard work to go home without something.

"Get out of here. She's coming with us, and if you know what is good for you, you'll head back to whatever rock you crawled out from under," the lead vampire said. Jackson glared at him before finally walking past them, leaving his victim for the night behind.

This complicated things greatly. He couldn't kill, and then clean up his mess. Part of the ritual was for someone to *discover* the mess. That was the second best part! The best part was the moment that his victim realizes that he is going to kill her.

As he walked home in anger, his mind was clouded and distracted. He was almost home to his residence in the Garden District, when he felt an odd presence. Turning to look in all directions, he didn't see anyone, and chalked it up to him being jittery from the engagement with the vampires moments ago. Clicking the key into the lock of his house, he opened the door, and placed his keys and wallet on the table in the foyer.

It would take some serious thought and planning to figure out what to do next. He needed to kill, and it had to be soon. He had already contemplated moving to a new city, because he knew these encounters would only continue. But, he liked how easy it was to pluck a victim from the French Quarter at the same time. Having already done research on a handful of other cities around the world before he settled on New Orleans, he had a few places in mind if things got worse. Sighing, he went over to his laptop and turned it on to dig deeper on some of those cities. These vampires and covens were turning out to be a real pain in Jackson's ass.

# Chapter 9

I got the call sometime after four in the morning from my Divine Assassin buddy Mark that he had huge news for me. "Come over to our rental immediately, Skyy!" he exclaimed over the phone with excitement.

"I'll be right there, hold your horses!" I told him, laughing as I hung up. Still dressed in case we needed to leave at a moment's notice, I slipped on my shoes and grabbed Aiden. "We need to run over to the rental real fast sweetie," I told him, as I helped him up off the couch and kissed his cheek.

There weren't many Divine Assassins in the house at the moment, since they were all out on the streets looking for signs of our enemies. Mark was smiling from ear to ear when he saw me walk in. He was with his new partner, a man named Jacob. I didn't know him too well, but he seemed decent enough, and was always civil with me, so that made him okay in my book.

Aiden and I were holding hands, and he broke away to shake Mark's hand before guiding me over to the small couch in the living room to sit down with me. "Good to see you, Mark," he said in a friendly tone.

"You as well, Aiden. Okay, are you guys ready for this!?" he said. I was waiting for a drum roll to start with the way he was building up to whatever it was he wanted to tell us. Smiling at him, I nodded my head and spun my hand around in the air telling him to get to the point already.

"We were out on the streets tonight, and saw a fellow in a bar on Bourbon Street that fit Jack's description. He was there for hours and hours, buying drinks for a young girl who was alone, which was even more suspicious, so we stuck around," he started out. I instantly sat up and scooted forward on the couch, waiting to hear more.

"Finally, he left the bar with her, and we put on our invisibility spell and followed him from a safe distance. Sure enough, it was Jack! He was stopped by six vampires, and they exchanged some words. The covens here are pissed, and want him to stop killing in public. They took the girl from him, and he walked away...all the way to his house, which is in the Garden District!" he exclaimed.

I jumped out of my seat, and grabbed the top of my head in disbelief. "What! Are you serious!?" I yelled out.

"I am dead serious. AND, here is the best part. He was so distracted from the encounter with the vampires, that Jacob here was able to perform a scrying spell on him, so we can track him at any time now. All we need to do now is wait for the right time to attack!"

I looked over at Aiden, who was now standing by my side. He smiled at me, and took my hand in his once more, squeezing it. "This is what we have been waiting for, Skyy! Good work guys, this is huge!" he congratulated them.

"Indeed, good work Mark! We'll call together a meeting with our vampires immediately and come up with a plan that works for us. We will strike as a team when the time is right, Divine Assassins, and vampires together!" I told him.

"We also have some more news. The vampire Claude was spotted at several different locations tonight in the French Quarter. He was only with one other vampire. It seems like the events that took place in the club didn't stop him from going out and about so soon," Mark informed us.

"Good. The idiot is too stupid to know what is best for him. It will make getting to him, and hopefully Bathory, easier," Aiden replied.

Nodding at him, I was almost giddy from excitement, and couldn't contain myself. "This all seems too good to be true! I am hoping that we can at least take care of Jack without complications. If that is all you have for us, Mark, we'll take off with lightning speed to tell our vampires the great news!"

"Yep, that's it, Skyy! Couldn't wait to tell you. We were sitting there all night hoping for the best, watchin' the creep make his moves on that poor girl. I know she left with other vampires, but I hope at least she won't lose her life."

"I don't know about that, and I don't even want to think about it right now. We need to focus on the good news. I'll be in touch very soon Mark. Thanks again for the awesome work tonight!" I said, as I gave him a high five on the way towards the door.

Aiden and I smiled at each other as we flew with great haste back to our rental house. I flung the door open and called out to the entire house, "Great news, everyone! Come down to the living room right away!"

In less than a minute, the entire house of vampires were assembled before Aiden and me. They could tell by my smile that it was good news. I am sure they were feeling the same way I was waiting for Mark to tell us, so I didn't waste any time. I let them in on the entire story, and loved watching their faces light up when I got to the part about the tracking spell.

They were all just as excited as we were. "Finding him has been the hardest part. If we know exactly where he will be from now on, all we have to do is wait for the time to strike," Lucius said.

"Exactly! And since we know that Claude is out and about already, I think it's best that we let the Divine Assassins continue to monitor him incognito. We should make killing Jack our number one priority, and walking into a trap set by Claude wouldn't be good," I presented to the room, and they all agreed with me.

Arabella, in a rare moment of speaking, chimed in. "I can't wait for you to take him out. I would love to be there when you do. I know that you guys don't want me out on the streets for obvious reasons right now, but watching him die would give me peace," she said softly to the room, all the while keeping her eyes averted to the carpet.

My heart went out to her, and I looked to Lucius, for whatever reason, for the answer. Raising my eyebrows to him in question, he finally spoke. "If we think that it is something you can safely participate in, you can most certainly come along, Arabella. Nobody deserves to see justice served to Jack more than you do," he said, kindly.

Arabella didn't speak, but just smiled and nodded her head once in thanks. The sun was about to rise for the morning, and Jack was in for the night. We'd have to wait until tomorrow night to see what would happen. We all stayed in the living room, talking and planning for another hour or so, before everyone went to their rooms. Ridley went over to the other rental house to meet with the Divine Assassins, and I decided I would venture out into the sunlight again to see what would happen.

Aiden, of course, was not happy. We were in our bedroom, and I was changing into something cooler. Ruffling through my suitcase that I still had not fully unpacked, I pulled out a black tank top and some cute white shorts, put them on, and tied my long hair up in a ponytail. Aiden was arguing with me the whole time.

"Skyy, we don't have any idea how this magic works. If something were to happen to you…" he said, as he let the sentence trail off. I could see him starting to get choked up, and embraced him.

"I know, Aiden. We have had this conversation about sixty times in the last couple of days. It scares me too, but it is also something that we can use to our advantage. We can't just think of ourselves here, I am doing this to hopefully help all of us. Just stand by my side, and I will tell you when I have had enough in the sun. I won't push myself, I promise. Okay?" I said, as I looked up at his handsome face.

He looked down at me with total admiration and love. It was killing him to see me in danger once again. I felt terrible that I brought him so much worry, especially since he led such a quiet life up until he met me. "You're right Skyy, but it doesn't mean I have to like it. You're my entire world, milady. I'll trust your judgement, if that is what you wish."

It brought tears to my eyes when he said I was his entire world. Wrapping my arms around him even tighter, I buried my face in his chest and said, "I love you so much, Aiden." He kissed the top of my head, and I could tell he was shedding a couple of tears as well. We embraced one another in total silence for a few more moments, before heading to the patio door.

Aiden took my hand in his, and guided me out into the sunlight. I didn't plan on staying out here more than a few minutes, if that. The grass was still covered in dew from the morning, and it was cool on my bare feet. My skin, however, quickly began to heat up. Much faster than the previous times. Barely making it thirty seconds, I told Aiden I had enough, and he whisked me back inside before I felt faint.

"Okay. That was much faster this time, but I didn't get to the point I was exhausted. If I can do this a couple times today, we can see what happens. I don't want to test out the magic again in the house, we'll go somewhere remote, preferably where there is water, and experiment later," I said to Aiden, as he heated some blood for me.

I drank the blood down quickly, and was feeling back to normal in no time. If my ability to be out in the sun was being diminished, this would really suck. I loved that we could all be out in the sunlight, especially since the daytime was the only time we knew we were one hundred percent safe from any vampire enemies.

Aiden was especially concerned for me, and I wanted to spend some alone time with him before my next round in the sunlight. I hopped up off of the barstool I was sitting on in the kitchen, and asked him if he wanted to spend the rest of the morning cuddling in bed. Without hesitation, he smiled at me and nodded his head.

Stripping out of all of our clothes, we slid between the cool sheets, and cuddled in between making love for several hours. It was well into the afternoon now, and I wanted to try to go out in the sun one more time before it got dark, so we put our clothes back on, and went back outside.

Once again, I was only able to withstand it for about thirty seconds, before coming back inside. My hands, and eyes got brighter and brighter each time. We waited for the sun to go down, and Lucius suggested that he and Sergei try to teach me how they can control their fire. Aiden drove us down to a small lake in the woods that they had scouted out. Making sure there was no chance any humans were around, we began the lesson.

Sergei, with his broken English, knew much more than Lucius, who had only recently started to learn how to control his odd powers. Sergei told me about meditation, and how to visualize what I wanted to do with my sunlight. "Like this," he said, as fire ignited from his hand. He directed it out from him in a line out over the water, then put it out as quickly as he had lit it. I tried, and tried to get the sun to ignite without friction, and it just didn't happen. "That's ok, maybe your power works differently from ours," Sergei said, and smiled at me reassuringly.

Lucius was standing next to me, lighting his hands on fire, and extinguishing them over and over. He was still practicing, and just like my sunlight, it wasn't too safe to do it inside. "Lookin' good, Lucius!" I called out to him as I gave him the thumbs up sign. He smiled back at me as he lit his hands up again, then threw a fireball into the water.

Aiden was sitting back on a dead tree stump watching all of us. I looked back at him, and said "Well, here goes nothing." Snapping my fingers together once was all it took this time. I almost got blown back onto my ass with the power that came out of me. The woods around us lit up, as a massive ball of sunlight hovered between my hands. It was easily the size of a basketball, much bigger than the smaller ball of mist from yesterday. "Whoa," I whispered.

"Skyy! That is amazing!" Sergei yelled out to me. They had all backed off considerably from me, for good reason. Though the illuminated ball was surrounded by mist, the ball itself was solid now. "I can feel the heat emanating off of it from over here!" Sergei called out again. He was easily thirty feet away from me. I didn't feel a thing, and I was right on top of it.

"This thing can probably be seen from outer space, I shouldn't hang on to this for too long, or we might draw attention to ourselves," I said, getting worried about being seen.

Lucius and Sergei agreed with me, and I decided to fling it into the lake. Using a decent amount of force, I tossed it towards the water, and watched in horror as it went under the water, but didn't extinguish. The lake was bubbling like a cauldron from the heat of the magical energy. "Holy shit! Now what?!" I exclaimed.

Aiden was on his feet, and the men all rushed over to my side watching the ball glow under the water. "See if you can guide it back to you!" Lucius suggested, in a panic.

"How?!" I asked him.

"Concentrate. Call out to it with your mind. It is how I control the fire. It's all I can suggest," he said quickly.

I tried to do as he instructed, and nothing happened. Stupidly, I snapped my fingers again, thinking that it might come back to me, but instead I summoned another large ball of energy. "Crap!" I yelled out. Running out of ideas, I used one of my hands to pull at the one in the lake, as if I were reeling in a fish. Surprisingly it worked! It floated up out of the water, and slowly glided back to me. Once it arrived, it gelled together with the second ball, to form a gigantic mass.

The area around us was illuminated even more now, and I knew we would draw attention to ourselves. If a plane flew anywhere near this area, they would surely see it. The men had backed off again from the heat. Running out of ideas for how to get rid of the magic safely, I tried bringing my hands together.

The tension was extreme, but I pushed back as hard as I could. The ball of energy was shrinking in size! I concentrated as hard as I could, and used all my physical strength to extinguish the magic. Finally, my hands came together, and the light was gone. "Well, that was better than setting the woods on fire," I laughed. The men all agreed, and laughed with me.

Aiden rushed to my side, and inspected me. "Do you feel alright?" he asked, concerned for my well-being.

"Actually, I feel great. Almost energized."

"That was an amazing sight, Skyy. You can control it now, and I bet with more practice you can figure out how to do even more with it!" Lucius exclaimed.

I could tell that Aiden was torn on whether he was happy for me, or worried for me. Taking his hand into mind, I squeezed it tightly for reassurance. "Your hand is quite warm," he said, as he let it go.

"Sorry," I said, as I looked down at my hands. They were glowing brightly in the darkness of the woods. "We should probably get out of here." The men agreed, and we piled back into the SUV to head home.

Planning on staying in again tonight and wait on the Divine Assassins to check in with us, Aiden and I headed back up to our bedroom to settle in for a while. Once we were in each other's arms, he smiled at me and said, "Don't set the bed on fire, milady." I chuckled, and kissed him softly.

# Chapter 10

Ridley was at the Divine Assassin's rental house, when he got a call from Aimee. He hesitated for a few seconds, before answering. "Hello?" he said, as he placed the phone to his ear.

"Ridley! Hi, it's Aimee," came the bubbly voice from the other end.

"Hi, Aimee. How's it going?"

"Good! I was wondering if you had plans for the day?" she asked, with hope in her voice.

Ridley knew that Skyy would kill him if he got Aimee wrapped up in things. But he was torn, because he genuinely liked her. Since she was over at the other house for the day, he figured what she didn't know wouldn't hurt her.

"No, I am free. Why?" he replied, taking a bold step towards the unknown.

"Would you like to come over to my house for lunch and a movie?" she asked him. He could tell that she was just as nervous as he was.

"Sure, that sounds great. What time?"

"You can come by any time. I'll make some pasta salad and sandwiches," she told him cheerfully.

"Sounds good! I'll get ready, and leave the house in about fifteen minutes," he told her.

Ridley hung up, and looked down at his clothes. He was wearing one of the outfits Skyy had helped him pick out. Some cargo shorts, and a t-shirt with a band he had never heard of on the front of it. He was not comfortable in these clothes, but figured he looked presentable enough. Skyy had also insisted on him getting a new hairstyle, and he glanced at his tousled hair in the mirror as he grabbed a set of car keys off the foyer table. The Divine Assassins had several rental cars for their work in New Orleans. He hoped they didn't mind if he borrowed one for a couple of hours.

He knew where she lived from the time they drove her home. It wasn't too far from the French Quarter, and he was there in no time. It was a small house, and she lived alone. He knocked on the door, and heard a small dog bark from behind it. Aimee opened the door and smiled at Ridley, and the source of barking was right behind her. A little tan and white Lhasa Apso wagged her tail happily as Aimee stepped aside and let Ridley in.

Immediately, he noticed that her once green hair, was now all black. Her eyebrow ring and small nose stud were also missing. She stood up on her tip toes to give Ridley a welcoming hug, which he gladly returned. "What happened to the green hair?" he said, as he pointed to her head.

Aimee shrugged her shoulders. "I dunno, I was kind of tired of always having to dye it. The colors fade fast. Do you like it?"

Ridley nodded to her, and smiled. "Yes, black looks great on you!" he replied sincerely. She guided him into her house, and walked into the kitchen. It was a very clean, and well-kept house that was small, but cozy. He was shocked that her style for interior decorating was totally different than her appearance. He figured it would be decorated in gothic type decorations, but instead it was mostly neutral colors, with lots of pictures of her friends and family all over the walls. He walked around the living room looking at all the photos while she made sandwiches.

She had a big family from the looks of it, and lots of friends. Something he had neither of. Aimee hadn't always had the piercings and colored hair. She was a very pretty girl, and it looked like her natural hair color was a dark brown. Her blue eyes were crystal clear, and always happy. "Great pictures. You have a big family!" he said, attempting to start a conversation.

She came out into the living room with two sandwiches that she placed on a large coffee table in front of the couch. "Yes indeed! I have five brothers, and ten cousins. Plenty of nieces and nephews, since I am the baby in the family. What would you like to drink?" she asked.

"Oh, water is fine. Thank you."

He sat down on the comfortable, well lived-in couch, and the little dog jumped up in his lap right away. She started licking his arm, which made him smile. Aimee came back with two bottles of water, and tried to shoo the dog away. "Cookie! Get down!" she scolded. The dog ignored her.

Ridley laughed. "It's okay. I love dogs. She can stay up here."

Aimee rolled her eyes as she sat on the other end of the couch. "I don't think she is giving you a choice. She is a stubborn little thing. But I love her," she said, as she ruffled the fur on Cookie's head. "So, I have a new horror movie I have been dying to watch. But if you don't like that, we can watch something else. Your choice!"

"Horror is fine. I'll watch just about anything. I don't get much time to myself to watch movies," he said.

"So what is it that you do, exactly?" Aimee asked, as she took a bite of her sandwich.

Ridley hadn't really thought this far ahead. Every other time they were together, they were in noisy clubs or bars and didn't get much of a chance to talk to each other about important things. There was so much about his life that he could never tell her, and it killed him. He really liked Aimee, and it was finally sinking in that Skyy was right. He could never be with her.

"I am a computer technician, my family owns a company that runs surveillance," he said, stretching the truth. It was *mostly* true.

"Oh neat. Are you an only child?" she asked, continuing with the personal things.

"I wasn't. I had a sister, but she passed away," he replied, thinking back on his painful past.

"Oh no, I am so sorry Ridley. I didn't mean to bring up bad memories," she said sincerely, as she reached out to touch his forearm.

He shook his head to reassure her. "No, it's fine. It was a long time ago. My mother and her are both gone. But we don't have to talk about depressing things," he said, trying to change the subject so he wouldn't have to answer any more difficult questions.

"So how do you like living here in New Orleans? The guys you're here with, are they all part of your company as well?" she said, unknowingly going right back to the sticky subject. Ridley hated lying, but he couldn't tell her the truth.

"I am not sure what I think of New Orleans. As I am sure you can tell, I am not really the going out type of guy. The first time I ever had a drink was with you the other night. So, it is very different than what I am used to. The architecture is beautiful. And, yes the people with me all work for my company," he said, hoping she wouldn't ask more about them.

Aimee giggled at his reply. "Yes, I gathered that from the very first time I met you. You definitely fit the computer technician role. For what it's worth, I think you looked just as handsome before your makeover," she said, as she blushed.

This, in turn, made Ridley blush. He had never really dated anyone, because he never wanted to risk getting them killed by Bathory, as his mother and sister had been. His work with the Divine Assassins kept him busy enough. And he certainly never thought of himself as handsome. He looked like he was still in his twenties, and even though he wasn't stylish, he always thought of himself as kind of plain.

But, seeing as he was secluded away at headquarters, away from the general public most of the time, he never really had a chance to see what women thought. "Thank you, Aimee. I'm certainly not the most stylish person on the planet. Skyy means well, but this look isn't really me," he said, as he looked down at his band shirt.

"What, you don't like Disturbed?" she said, as she laughed again.

"Honestly, I have never even heard of them. Laugh it up," he said as he chuckled.

"That is too cute. I think I have some of their music, if you want to listen to it," Aimee said, as she scooted closer to him on the couch. The sandwich was placed on the table, and forgotten.

"Sure. At least then I can say I have heard it when people ask me if I like them," Ridley replied. Aimee pulled her phone out of her pocket, and put on one of the bands albums. She laughed as she watched Ridley's reaction. He was a good sport about it, and listened to several songs. Eventually, it grew on him, and he actually enjoyed the music. Aimee was even closer to him now, facing towards him on the couch, with her legs crossed in front of her. They bobbed their heads with the rhythm.

Ridley loved the way she made him feel. She accepted him, even though he was a geek. She was funny, pretty, and smart. For a short moment, he imagined what it would be like if he could actually date her. He'd never even kissed a girl before, and stared at Aimee's adorable mouth as she talked about her favorite bands, dreaming of what it would be like to be happy again.

His family had been taken away from him decades ago, and he devoted his entire life to the Divine Assassins and hunting down Bathory. A few of the men were married, and their wives knew the whole story. He wondered how Aimee might react if she knew the truth. Ridley also wondered if he would stay with the Divine Assassins after they killed Bathory once and for all if he had someone special in his life.

He picked up his sandwich that she had made for him over an hour ago, and ate it so that he wouldn't seem rude. She never finished hers, and kept introducing him to new songs and bands as he ate. Ridley was never big on heavy metal, but it was growing on him. He could endure it, if it meant getting closer to Aimee.

One of the questions that had been on his mind, was why she didn't have a boyfriend. He actually didn't even know *if* she did or not. He finally worked up the courage to ask. "You don't have a boyfriend?" he said quietly, without making eye contact.

Aimee's face got sad at the mention of a boyfriend. She looked down at her phone that she was holding in her hands, and turned down the volume of the music so they could talk. "No. I was with someone for almost a year, and I found out he was cheating on me. I have not dated since then. He was a bad-boy; long hair, motorcycle...the works. Broke my heart."

"I'm so sorry Aimee. I shouldn't have brought it up." Ridley felt like an idiot for asking now. He placed his empty plate on the coffee table.

"No, don't be sorry! It was almost three years ago. I'm over it now, but it took me a while to get past it. How about you?" she asked, wanting to know more personal information about him.

"Oh. Umm. No...no girlfriend here," was his nervous reply.

Aimee laughed at his cute reply. "You sure about that?" she poked fun at him.

He blew out air he didn't know he had been holding, and replied. "Yes, I am positive. I don't have much time for dating, as you can see."

"Well, you're here, aren't you? I guess you have more time than you might think," she said, in a flirtatious way.

Ridley blushed again. "So, is this an official date?" he ventured to ask.

"Do you want it to be?" she replied, flirting again. She smirked at him with her cute mouth, and it made his heart skip a beat.

He knew he should say "no!" and could hear Skyy yelling at him in his mind. But his heart took over, and he got the courage to look her in her beautiful blue eyes, and say "Yes."

She gave him a full smile now, and took his large hand into her tiny one. "Good. Our first official date! How exciting!" Ridley laughed as he looked down at their intertwined fingers. He wanted this more than anything in the world.

They continued to listen to music for a little while longer, before Aimee popped in the horror movie. She got a big, warm blanket and covered up their legs with it before she snuggled in to Ridley's side. He placed his arm around her, and smiled. Ironically, the movie was about vampires, and was so far off from the reality that it made him laugh. Aimee loved it though, and once it was over they discussed it.

"So, what did you think about the movie?" she asked, as she took his hand that was draped over her shoulder into hers once more. She played with his fingers and caressed his hand with hers as they talked.

"Well, it was pretty corny. I mean, the special effects were good, but the vampires were pretty hokey."

"Really?! I thought they looked cool! Cooler than the nerds who walk around the French Quarter dressed up like vampires. It'd be awesome if they really existed," she said, fantasizing.

Ridley couldn't believe how this conversation was progressing. He wanted to change the subject as soon as possible. Thankfully he didn't have to, she did it herself. "Crap, I have to be at work in about an hour. Lost track of time."

"Oh, I can get out of your hair if you need to get ready," Ridley replied.

"No, it's okay! I'd love for you to stay with me until I have to go. I am ready, just need to put shoes on. We have an hour," she told him. They put on the TV and snuggled up on the couch again until it was time for her to leave for work. Ridley had a fantastic time, and was on cloud nine.

"I can drive you to work, if you'd like? What time do you get off? I can probably give you a ride home too," he said, wanting to see her again. He'd deal with Skyy when the time came.

"Oh? A second date so soon?" she teased, as she put her shoes on by the front door. Ridley blushed and put his hands in his pocket. Cookie was anxiously waiting to see if she'd get to come along on the adventure outside the house.

"Yes, I'd love a second date," he said, shyly.

Aimee came over to Ridley, and in a brave moment, placed her hands gently on his hips. He was much taller than her, and it made her feel safe. He was a good guy, and the total opposite of her ex. She knew that he would never cheat on her, without even having to think twice about it. He was a kind gentleman. And he had no idea how cute he was either. Behind the geeky clothing and hair, was a handsome guy, and she thought to herself how lucky she would be if he chose to be with her.

She stood up on her tip toes once more and gazed into his eyes. "I'd love a second date too," she whispered to him, as she moved her lips closer to his. Ridley shut his eyes, and let her soft lips touch his. His heart was beating quickly in his chest, and he hoped she couldn't hear it and tell how nervous he was.

Her adorable mouth gently kissed his, and then she deepened the kiss once she felt his hands rise to her mid-back. Ridley embraced her into his arms, and pulled her closer to him. He smelled so good, and the moment felt perfect to both of them. They made out like two teenagers on prom night, before Ridley finally broke away, and whispered, "You're going to be late for work."

Aimee sighed as she wrapped her arms around Ridley and held on to him. "I don't care. It's worth it."

Eventually they made their way out to Ridley's car. It was already dark out, and Aimee had to be at the clothing store at seven. They held hands the entire way to the French Quarter, and he parallel parked in the street outside of the store to drop her off. She leaned over in the seat to kiss him once more, which turned into another make out session. Finally, she opened the door, and leaned into the window to tell him what time to pick her up.

"I get off at midnight, if that is too late, I can always bum a ride home from a friend who works down the street. I really enjoyed our first date, Ridley."

"Midnight isn't too late. I will see you then. I enjoyed it as well. Thank you for lunch, too," he said, as he waved goodbye to her.

He pulled into the street, with a huge smile on his face. What he failed to see, was the vampire watching them from across the street as he dropped her off. He recognized Ridley right away, and called Claude. He was instructed to grab Aimee, and let Ridley leave. They planned on using her to get to Skyy.

Aimee never even made it inside the clothing store. She was silenced, and mind-whammied the moment that Ridley left. She didn't put up a fight, and went with the vampire.

# Chapter 11

Ridley went back up to the French Quarter at a little before midnight to pick up Aimee. He was puzzled when he walked in the store, and saw another sales associate working the counter. "Hi, is Aimee here?" he asked.

The guy was pissed off. "I don't know where she is! She never made it in for her shift, and won't answer her phone, been here for twelve fucking hours now."

Ridley instantly panicked. He pulled his phone out of his pocket, and dialed her number as he walked back out to his car that was parked in the street. Someone picked up, but it wasn't Aimee.

"We've been waiting all night for you to call, Ridley. Don't worry, Aimee is safe, and will stay safe as long as you cooperate. She sure does taste good though," the man on the other end taunted.

Ridley's stomach dropped and he felt sick. His worse fear was coming true, and they were barely even dating before it happened.

"Speechless, I see. Well, let me tell you what we want. You get in touch with your vampire friend, Skyy, and meet us tonight at this address. If all goes well, we'll exchange Aimee for Skyy." The vampire on the other end didn't even give Ridley a chance to reply before he hung up. A moment later, he received a text with the address.

Now…how was he going to tell all of this to Skyy?

• • •

Ridley placed his hand over the welt that was forming on his upper arm where I had smacked him. "You dumb ass! I can't believe this!" I screamed out at him in anger. "I *TOLD* you not to get that poor girl involved in any of this!"

Aiden came over to my side and moved me away from Ridley gently. "Skyy, calm down. I am sure he didn't intentionally mean to get her into trouble. As we can all see, he cares about her. Let's think this through without yelling at one another," he said kindly.

"Oh my God, Aiden! She could potentially get killed! I told him to stay away from her! Her cousin is going to kill us all for this! I can't calmly address this situation! Now they want to exchange me for her, and what choice do I have? I can't let her die!" I screamed out at him. I was beyond pissed off at Ridley, and wanted to kick him in the nuts for his stupid ass decision.

"They want to exchange you for her. That won't happen. We'll all go together, and they will be sorry they abducted her when it's all said and done," Lucius chimed in from the hallway, as he walked into the room.

He whistled through his teeth when he saw the welt on Ridley's arm. "She got you good, huh?"

Ridley knew better than to say anything, or else he'd get whacked by me once more. He stood there without saying a word, staring at the carpet.

"Tell your men to get ready, they will follow us for backup in the event we need it. Who knows what we will walk in to, but we will be prepared as best we can. There is no choice now, we have to get Aimee out of there safely," Lucius ordered to Ridley. He nodded, and left for the other rental house to inform the Divine Assassins.

I was pacing the room like a madwoman. I was so pissed, but deep down inside I couldn't blame Ridley. I knew he had feelings for Aimee from the first day he met her. I was mad because I didn't want to see anything happen to her. And, if we got her out alive, we'd have to make the decision to let her know about us, or wipe her mind.

"Come on, Skyy. Let's go get you changed into something so we can leave here as soon as they are ready," Aiden said to me, as he guided me back to our room. I followed his orders, and put on some black leggings, a tight black baby doll t-shirt, and some combat boots. I didn't feel the need to take my magical sword with me, because I felt like the magical sunlight would probably do the trick.

Fiona braided my long hair as we waited for the Divine Assassins to get geared up and ready. We had six carloads of people and vampires by the time it was all said and done. We navigated to the address that they had texted to Ridley, and thankfully it was in a secluded area. We pulled up into the gravel driveway of a tiny little shack of a house in the middle of nowhere.

I saw my good friend Claude immediately. He was with at least a dozen other vampires that we could see from the outside of the house. Who knew how many were inside? My eyes were scanning the area looking for Bathory, but I didn't see her.

Aiden took my hand into his, and the other vampires lined up right behind us. The Divine Assassins set up a perimeter outside the area. "Where is Aimee?" I called out to Claude.

"She is inside. Come with us, and leave the others here," he yelled back to me.

Aiden spoke up before I could. "Not going to happen, buddy. I go where she goes."

He laughed. "Even better. Come on inside with her, if you dare."

We looked back at our friends, and they knew to be on alert. With no other choice, we walked up to the house, and followed Claude inside. I saw Aimee right away. They had her gagged, and bound up to a chair. Her face was red and swollen from crying, and her eyes were panicked. She saw me walk in and started struggling against her bonds. "It's ok Aimee. We're getting you out of here. Ridley is outside, waiting for you," I told her, trying to comfort her.

I could see several wounds on her arms and neck where the vampires had fed from her. I planned on killing every single one of the pieces of shit for it too. Once I was inside, I could see there were probably fifteen vampires' total, and Bathory was nowhere to be seen.

"Where is your boss, Claude?" I said, taunting him.

"This is between you, and me. She doesn't tell me what to do," he replied, taking my bait. He was filled with anger, and wanted revenge…that much was obvious.

"What a shame. I've missed her so much."

Claude nodded to a vampire behind us, and in the blink of an eye he was upon Aiden. "I told you that I would take your love from you one day. I keep my promises," he said, menacingly.

I *tsked* at the vampire holding on to Aiden. He released him for a brief moment to back away from me. "I wouldn't do that if I were you," I said, as I reached out and touched him. He turned into a pile of ash seconds later. I stepped onto the ashes, and took Aiden's hand.

"Why does he not burn to ash when you touch him?!" Claude screamed out at me, enraged. His bald head was shining under the bright lights in the room, and I could see veins popping out under the skin he was so mad.

"Wouldn't you like to know?" I replied with a smirk. "Come closer and I'll show you."

He went to Aimee's side, and bit into her neck fiercely. I could see blood pouring out the sides of his mouth as he sucked on her. Cringing, I let go of Aiden's hands, and snapped my fingers. My magical ball of energy illuminated before me.

That caught his attention. He looked up from Aimee, blood dripping from his mouth, and stopped in his tracks. "What the hell?" he murmured. Smelling Aimee's blood was making me uncomfortable. I wanted to end this right away, and get out of here with her so that we could tend to her wounds.

"Give me Aimee, and I will come with you. Try anything funny, and I will burn you, and this house, to ash. I don't even have to touch you, either," I demanded. Aiden had backed off from me because of the heat.

Claude was scared, and I could see it in his eyes. He did as I told him, and released Aimee. She flew into Aiden's arms, and he walked her outside to Lucius, who instantly started to tend her wounds. Now that she was safe, I pushed my magical energy back into my hands, so that Claude would think I was cooperating.

His vampire minions that were with him moved closer to me, thinking that they would escort me out of there. None of them would touch me, which was smart. As soon as they got close enough, I snapped my fingers once more, and directed my ball of sunlight out towards them. I closed my eyes this time, to avoid being blinded. The moment it came in contact with the vampires, it burst into action. Even with my eyelids closed the light was bright. I opened my eyes once I knew it was safe, and looked around the room.

I took out ten of the fifteen vampires in one hit. Claude and the rest of the vampires were on the floor covering their eyes. I knew they were temporarily blinded. Walking over to his minions, I touched each of them one by one, turning them to ash with a simple touch of my hand. All that was left was Claude. Waiting patiently for his vision to come back, I took a seat in one of the chairs nonchalantly.

When he looked around the room, terror came over his face. I had killed fourteen of his men, plus his wife and sister-in-law, and the other vampires in the nightclub. "You are in no place to negotiate with me, you fool. I can kill you from a mile away, so don't forget that. Tell your boss that I want to meet with her. You have Ridley's number, text me when you have a location. If you don't, I will find you and kill you, but it won't be a fast death. I have a lot more tricks up my sleeve that you have no idea about," I threatened him.

Claude hauled ass out of the shack with lightning speed. I walked out the front door smiling, and greeted my friends. "The situation is handled. We're good to go."

Aimee was sitting in the trunk area of our SUV, with Ridley right by her side. She was crying hysterically, and he was rubbing her back and comforting her. Walking over to them, I wasn't really sure what to say to Aimee. I supposed apologizing would be a good start. "I am so sorry this happened to you, Aimee. I told Ridley not to go around you, so that you would never come into harm's way. He just likes you so much, he didn't listen," I joked, trying to get a smile out of her.

It worked, and she looked up at me with her tear-soaked face and smiled. She was visibly trembling, and for good reason. "So, I guess the 'family business' thing was all made up?" she said as she looked at Ridley.

"No, it's not made up. It's all true, mostly. I really am the computer guy for the business, but we don't operate like most businesses do. We do run surveillance, that part wasn't a lie either," he said, trying to defend himself.

I let the two of them work things out, and took Lucius aside. "Did you give her some blood to heal her wounds? I noticed they are all healed up."

He nodded at me. "Yes, I had to. She was in desperate need of either emergency room attention, or vampire healing. I asked her permission first, of course."

I crossed my arms and thought about everything for a moment. "So, what do you think we should do about her? Wipe her memory, or fill her in?" I asked him, wanting to know his thoughts.

"She can't be left alone now, so we pretty much have to keep her with us. Let's get out of here, in case more back up arrives, and take her back to the house and explain things," was his answer.

We piled back into our cars, and left pretty quickly. Ridley sat in the backseat of our SUV, with his arms around Aimee, as Aiden drove, and I sat in the passenger seat. We were careful to watch that we weren't being followed, but I honestly think that I killed everyone Claude had in on his little plan. It was really weird to see Ridley in a romantic situation. I always thought of him as my nerdy partner.

Once we got to the house, we took her inside and gave her a blanket to wrap up in. She was still shaken up, and was being thrown into a world she had no idea about. I needed blood desperately, since I could still smell the blood that had dried on her clothing from the attacks.

We introduced her to everyone, and Arabella smiled kindly at her. I think she was happy to have someone else around her age that could relate to being thrown into this weird situation. She will still having a hard time adjusting to her new life. "I think we're about the same size, Aimee. Would you like me to get you something else to change in to, so you can get out of those bloodied clothes?"

Aimee gladly accepted her offer, and thanked her over and over again. We waited on her to take a quick shower, and to change into the clean clothes, then Ridley got her a glass of water. Once we were all settled in, Lucius took the lead and began to explain the whole story. He started out explaining that vampires were real, which I am sure she had already figured out after the encounter with Claude.

Then he moved on to tell her about Bathory, Jack the Ripper, what the Divine Assassins were, how Ridley fit into all of it, and the current situation. She took all of it in, and asked questions from time to time.

"Now for the bad news. Normally, when a human comes into contact with us when they weren't supposed to, we would wipe your memory of the event. You'd walk away none-the-wiser that we exist. But, since your life is in serious danger, we need you to stay here with us until this situation is handled. If you wish for us to wipe your memory after it is resolved, which could take quite some time, we will be happy to do it for you. Or you can remain with Ridley and our group, and be welcomed in with open arms," Lucius explained to her.

Aimee looked over at Ridley, who was sitting right up against her on the couch, caressing her back. "You guys realize that this is a LOT to take in, right?" she said.

We all agreed with her, and Arabella piped up. "Aimee, nobody can relate to you more than I can. Not too long ago, I was living a totally normal life, just like you. I was in University, had everything I could ever want. Jack the Ripper attacked me, and almost killed me. If it weren't for Skyy and her friends here, I would be dead. Some days I wonder if I would have been better off that way, but I am slowly becoming used to my new life.

This is a great bunch of people, trust me when I say they will keep you safe."

"Well, I don't know what to say. Thank you is a good place to start. If it weren't for you guys, I would probably be dead right now. Can I go home eventually, and get some clothes? What about work?" she asked.

"Of course, we can take you over to your house tomorrow in the daylight. The enemies we are hunting cannot go out in the sunlight, so we'll be safe during the day. As for work, if you are signed on for night shifts, I'd ask if they can be changed to day shifts. If not, you'll have to consider quitting. And of course, you can't talk to anyone about this," Lucius added.

"Well, actually…she can. Her cousin Pierce knows all about the vampire community. He is the one who told us he'd kill us if we got you wrapped up in any of this," I told her.

"Really?! Pierce knows about all of you, but kept me in the dark? That asshole."

I laughed at her reaction, and told her that he was cooperating with us, and seemed to be happy that we weren't like the covens.

"Trying to get a dayshift at the shop will be hard. I have always worked nights, and they are full on daytime employees," Aimee said sadly.

"Aimee, you don't ever have to worry about money as long as you're with us. If you need your rent to be paid, we are glad to help. There is no need to have to work right now, or ever again if you don't want to," Ridley explained to her. I watched her facial expression as he said this. She was really confused.

"Umm, I can't just take money from you guys. I am a hard worker, and I earn my keep. I can find a new job, it isn't a big deal. But thank you for the offer!"

"Actually, Aimee, it would be best for everyone if you didn't work right now. We can keep you safer if you don't," Lucius told her.

Her face sunk, and she looked at Ridley once more. "Okay. Well...I want to stay alive, so if you think this is for the best, then I will do as you ask. I'll definitely need help on my rent and car payment if that is the case."

"No problem at all. We will take care of all of that in the morning," Ridley said cheerfully, glad to be able to help her.

We talked with her for a while longer, before she started to yawn, and get tired. "You've had a really crazy night; we should let you get some sleep. We can talk more in the morning," I told her, as Aiden and I stood up to take our leave. All of the other vampires did the same thing, leaving her and Ridley alone in the living room. He had his own bedroom, and I would normally offer for her to share with Arabella, if it weren't for the fact that she couldn't be in the same room that long with a human and not lose it.

I listened in on Ridley's conversation with her and smiled. "I will go grab some pillows and take the couch. You can have my bed, though you will have to share the bathroom with Fiona and Christian."

Moments later I heard him walk down the hallway to his room, and could tell Aimee was right on his heels. "Please, Ridley. I don't want to be alone. Can I stay in here with you? There is no need for you to take the couch," she begged him. She was still terrified, and for good reason.

Aiden and I giggled as we heard Ridley stutter out an answer. "Umm, s-sure? I guess that is okay. I can sleep on the floor," he said shyly.

"We are both adults, aren't we? I think after making out several times today, that we can both agree we are attracted to each other. I promise I don't bite. We can share the bed, if you're okay with it," Aimee replied.

I could only imagine Ridley's face right now, and the two of us were cracking up laughing at this point. Ridley agreed, and I heard the springs of the bed squeak as they both climbed into the bed eventually. They began to talk about more private things that I didn't really need to listen in on, so I drowned the conversation out quickly. She fell asleep before too long, and I was thrilled for Ridley. He deserved happiness, and Aimee was great for him. If anyone could pull him out of his shell, it would be her. And now that she knew the whole truth, things would be easier on him.

I brushed my teeth, and shed my clothing before slipping between the sheets with Aiden. He was already naked, and eagerly awaiting me in bed. I scooted up to him, and kissed him. "That was us, not too long ago. You were so shy and scared. It was adorable," I told him, as I caressed his cheek. I noticed faint traces of the mist coming off of my fingers from the friction.

Thankfully he had closed his eyes before he could see it, and was enjoying my touch. "Yes, I was quite terrified of you. I wanted to make sure that I treated you with respect, but at the same time I wanted to be with you so bad. You were quite a tempting vixen, I must say," he teased.

"Hey, when I see something I like, I want to make sure I don't lose it," I joked.

"Don't worry Skyy, you have my heart forever. You'll never, ever, lose me," Aiden whispered, before kissing me passionately. We'd had sex numerous times over the last couple of days, and I knew that I wasn't going to ignite the sunlight in any other way than from my hands. I just had to be careful with how I touched him from now on. Which would suck. No more hand jobs I guess. After Bathory and Jack were taken care of, the first order of business with the Divine Assassins would be trying to undo this crazy magic for both Flavia, and myself.

We stayed up for several hours enjoying each other completely. The sun eventually rose, and I ventured out in it once more for a few seconds. Ridley and Aimee slept in for a very long time, and I decided to check in with Mark to see if there were any developments with Jack.

I dialed his number, and he answered with a cheerful "Hello!"

"Hi Mark. Just checking in to see how things are going with Jack," I replied back, just as cheerful.

"He hasn't left his house since the night the vampires encountered him in the street. We're hopeful that he'll leave tonight, since I am sure he has to feed. I'll let you know right away if we see him," he told me.

"We'll be ready."

I hung up with Mark, and wondered if Claude had talked to Bathory yet. They both must be reeling after the encounter last night. Smiling to myself thinking back on it, I patiently waited on Ridley to wake up so I could check his phone to see if Claude had contacted him.

They emerged from their room just before eleven in the morning. Fiona was quick to make Aimee feel at home, as she did for me months ago when I was in Aiden's mansion. "Let me make you some breakfast, dear! I made a special trip to the store, and got the ingredients for pancakes, bacon, and eggs! Sit down and enjoy some juice," she said, as she guided the two of them over to the kitchen table.

"Need a hand?" I asked her, offering to help.

"No, honey. You guys all just relax. I have something else fun planned for us girls after breakfast is done," she said, and winked at me. I could only imagine what it was. Knowing Fiona, it was something to do with beauty.

And, I was right. After breakfast, Aimee let Ridley take care of her rent and car payment, then she came back and took a shower, before meeting up with Fiona in the kitchen once more. I heard Ridley and her discussing things in their bedroom just before she came out. "Fiona is the sweetest lady ever. You'll love her. She wants to do something nice for you, so go and have some fun. You deserve it. I'll be right here waiting for you once you're done," he told her sweetly.

I smiled at Fiona when we heard him tell her that. Flavia and Arabella entered the kitchen shortly after that. Once all the girls were gathered around the table, she brought over a huge kit. As suspected, she had everything but the kitchen sink in there. "First, I have planned for us to have some manicures and pedicures! A team of nail techs from a local salon should be here any moment to pamper us in the privacy of our own home. There are plenty of polish colors in here to choose from, ladies. Pick your colors out, and we'll get started shortly!"

Fiona meant well, and I could see that Aimee was really excited, as well as Arabella. She had barely left the rental house since arriving in New Orleans, and the nails would be a nice treat for her. I waited for the others to choose their colors, before looking in her giant kit of expensive nail polishes, and picking a pretty, shimmery, light blue color.

The nail techs arrived shortly after that, and brought in all their own supplies. We sat back in our chairs and soaked our feet in the warm foot baths, and let them work their magic on our hands and feet. I declined the manicure part, for obvious reasons, but I had to admit, even though I wasn't big on pampering myself, this did feel pretty good. The techs worked on us for almost two hours, and then took their leave.

Fiona had asked Aimee what her favorite place to eat was, and ordered food from there. Christian went to pick it up for her while we were finishing up our nails, and she was beyond thrilled. "You guys are amazing. I can't believe it! This is so much fun!" she exclaimed, as she bit into a muffuletta sandwich.

Flavia, Arabella, and I all excused ourselves for our own "lunch" while she ate, and were back in no time. Fiona took a quick leave as well, and then informed us that the next round of our girl's day was a makeover. This came as no shock to me; Fiona wanted to get her hands on us any chance she got.

Out came another huge kit, this one filled with makeup from all over the world. Most of it was still unopened. "Now, we can do some waxing, eyebrows, and facials first. I have just received a shipment of this wonderful face scrub from France. You'll love it!" she exclaimed, as we moved into the master bathroom to slather our faces with all of her soaps, scrubs, and masks.

We were all having so much fun, it felt like a teenage sleep over. Flavia was beyond excited, and admitted this was her first experience with anything like this. "I am so out of touch with the modern world. This is wonderful Fiona," she said, as she sat on the edge of the Jacuzzi tub next to Arabella.

"Why are you out of touch with the modern world?" Aimee dared to ask.

"I was taken hostage, and held captive for centuries by a coven in China. I only recently escaped, and am still learning the ways of this new world," Flavia told her openly. She had been through hell and back, but she was one tough cookie. Behind closed doors, I knew that she still struggled, and Lucius was slowly but surely helping her along with his love and guidance.

"Oh my! That sounds awful, Flavia. I am so sorry," Aimee told her. "Is that where the skin thing came from?" she asked as she pointed to the several locations on Flavia's body that were glowing.

"Sort of. It was started by devices that the coven placed inside my body to keep me captive, and the Divine Assassins used a magical potion on me to remove them. This was the result."

"And what about your hands, and eyes, Skyy?" she asked, turning the questions to me.

I laughed, and said, "Well, it's a pretty crazy story. I don't even know how to explain it really. Essentially, I drank a potion to help me learn a sun protection spell, and in turn it is now letting me absorb actual sunlight. I can control concentrated forms of sun now."

Her eyes got as huge as saucers when I told her the story. "What! That is unreal!" she exclaimed.

"It is still all brand new, and I am trying to figure out how it works."

"Well, it looks awesome. Both of you look awesome."

We continued to talk and share stories, as Fiona went around to each of us to wax and tweeze our eyebrows. After the facials, she moved on to makeup. Each of us got her undivided attention as she worked her cosmetic skills on us. Then came the hair. Overall, we killed the entire day, and it was great.

Aimee couldn't stop thanking her enough. "This was such an amazing day; it was wonderful getting to know all of you better. Fiona, you're amazing, I love the makeup and hair!"

"We need to do this more often," Flavia chimed in. She was thrilled to death with how she looked, and couldn't stop checking herself out in the mirror. Her long, red hair that was so similar to mine, was curled and pinned up in a fancy updo. Fiona added in a cute, sparkly flower for added effect.

Fiona had straightened my hair, and did a waterfall braid with the top portion of it. I loved it. Arabella had requested a French braid, and Aimee's medium length black hair was done up like a 1940s pinup girl. It was adorable on her.

We parted ways to find each of our significant others, and as expected, I found Aiden working on his laptop in the den with Lucius. The two of them were deep in their work when Flavia and I walked in. They both whistled simultaneously when we walked in the room.

"Looking lovely, ladies," Lucius said, as Flavia climbed into his lap. He closed the lid on his laptop immediately, and kissed her. She wrapped her tiny arms around his large frame and snuggled with him. Aiden stood up and crossed the room to embrace me, kissing me before holding me at arm's length to get a good look at me.

"Stunning, milady."

"Thank you. We had a great time today, and Aimee got to know us all a lot better, which I hope makes her feel more comfortable about staying in the house with us," I explained to him.

"She is a really sweet girl," Flavia added in.

# Chapter 12

I could hear Fiona and Christian already getting it on in their room. They didn't waste any time. Ridley was in the kitchen cooking dinner for Aimee. Arabella was in her room, listening to music, most likely to drown out the sex coming from Christian's room. Sergei was outside meditating. We had a full house, and I once again reminded myself how lucky I was to have such an amazing group of people to call my allies and friends.

After drinking some blood in our room, Aiden and I settled in to watch a movie. We knew that it was highly likely that Mark would call us with news on Jack tonight, so we had to keep our clothes on for the most part. Aiden had already packed us a to-go knapsack with blood in it, in the event that we were out and I needed it.

Sure enough, around midnight, we got the call that Jack had emerged from his house in the Garden District. "He's heading right for the French Quarter."

Knowing that Claude had suffered major losses the night before, we felt that it was safe enough to risk venturing out tonight as a team. There was no news about the meeting I demanded with Bathory, which for now, might be a good thing. We could focus on Jack one hundred percent.

Aiden and I put our shoes on, and called out to the others to meet us downstairs right away. As promised, we told Arabella that she could come, and she thanked us before running off to get her shoes on as well.

That left Aimee. She didn't want to be left alone, and I told Ridley that he could stay behind with her. "Skyy! No! We are a team; I won't let you down on this. It is one of our biggest nights ever," he protested.

"Yeah, and your sweet girlfriend needs your emotional support. Sometimes you have to do what is needed. We have plenty of back up, Divine Assassins planted all over the French

Quarter to help. All of the vampires are with me. It's okay to sit this one out, Ridley," I told him.

I could tell he was between a rock and a hard place. I put my hand on his shoulder, and shared some advice. "Welcome to my world. Aiden worries sick about me on an hourly basis. Now you have someone in your life that is more important than anything else. You need to take care of her first."

He nodded his head at me in agreement. "Alright, Skyy. I know you're right, but I don't want to let either of you down. She is still very shaken up from last night, despite the wonderful day that you girls spent with her. Leaving her alone wouldn't be a good thing."

"I've got plenty of help...she's only got you. Stay with her, and comfort her."

"Okay. But call me immediately if you need help. Promise?" he said, looking at me seriously.

"Promise!"

We piled into the cars, and headed out to the French Quarter. Mark told me that Jack was on the outskirts, on a desolate street. The vampires didn't need cars to get around the area, so we parked ours on a side street several blocks away from where Jack was heading, and I told the Divine Assassins to track me through the ring they made for me when I was first initiated. All of the members of the Order have a tracking device implanted, so that they can track portals, and who is coming and going. Mine wouldn't stay under my skin because of my vampire healing abilities, so they crafted a ring I have to wear at all times instead.

They told us exactly where he was, and the group of us were off like a shot. The look on Jack's face when we surrounded him was priceless. He immediately looked for an opening to flee. I didn't want to chance lighting my magic in public; even though we were on such a desolate side street, there were still apartments and small businesses that were in the buildings. "Don't even try it," I told him.

His eyes lit up when he saw Arabella, instantly recognizing her. "Well, well," was all he said. He also knew she was our weakest link, and was on her in an instant, grabbing her from behind and restraining her. She was still too young, and since none of us had even begun to explain to her that vampires can develop special skills, she was little more than a resilient human. Jack dashed several feet away from the gap that she was standing in with her.

Even though he was outnumbered eight to one, he still kept it cool. His face never showed the panic he must have been feeling after the initial shock. His hazel eyes were glowing in the night, which was a dead giveaway. Arabella was terrified, and I could only imagine what she was thinking. She was back in the hands of the man who left her for dead.

Our group slowly moved towards him, and he kept slowly backing away from us. "Let her go, Jack," I called out to him.

He didn't speak a word, but his calculating eyes were bouncing between all of us waiting for our next move. He held Arabella in a choke hold in front of him, and she was struggling to get away to no avail. Thankfully, she wasn't screaming, because that would draw unnecessary attention to us. Ideally, we needed to get off of the streets, and dispose of Jack.

His next move caught us off-guard. He flung Arabella into us with amazing force, and catapulted himself up into the air, landing on the rooftop of the two-story buildings to our right. The French Quarter was comprised of alleyways and buildings that were all, for the most part, attached together. Jack took off into the night in the blink of an eye.

Christian, who had quickly picked up levitating and flying, launched himself up in the air and was gone. Lucius and Flavia followed. Sergei, Aiden, and Fiona stayed with Arabella and me, since we were the only two who could not levitate. Arabella couldn't even teleport short distances, and I was just getting the hang of it. Bringing her with us was now going to hold us back.

She was crying as we moved towards our car. "You're safe, Arabella. Get in, so we can catch up to them." I told her, as I hopped into the car. Aiden had it moving before we even closed the doors. Taking my phone out of the pocket of my jeans, I called Mark. "Where is he heading!?" I asked.

"Northwest, and he's moving very fast. We're already heading that way! Keep the line open, I will call out directions to you!" he said, with excitement.

"Can't this car go any faster?!" Sergei said, frustrated. Mark kept calling out directions to me over the phone, and Jack was still on the move, which meant none of my vampire friends had caught him yet. He was heading out of the French Quarter, and we navigated the cluttered streets to make our way out to Canal Street. Now risking getting pulled over if we started to speed, we got even more frustrated as Mark told us where he was.

"He is heading into a cemetery! If you're men can catch up to him in there, it would be perfect!" he told me.

I told Aiden to risk speeding, we could always mind-whammy the cop. Sergei opened the door to the car while we were doing close to seventy, and flew out of it. Apparently, he didn't want to wait. Fiona looked at me, and I knew she was thinking the same thing. "Go! If you can catch him faster, then do it Fi!"

Barely getting the words out, she followed Sergei's lead and opened the back door and jumped out. They were gone in the blink of an eye. Aiden pulled up to a cemetery that had an amazing tomb in the front; a manmade hill, with a beautiful deer statue on top of it. I would have time to admire it another day, right now we had to get to Jack. Aiden skidded to a stop just inside the gates, and we took off. Arabella would have to catch up, I wasn't going to miss our only chance at getting our hands on the slippery snake known as Jack the Ripper.

I could hear a battle taking place not far away. It sounded like cement being broken. We ran to the area it was coming from, and found Jack and Lucius dueling, with Flavia, Fiona, Sergei and Christian monitoring the perimeter. Lucius had slammed him into the side of a huge oven tomb that was made of cement, shattering it into pieces. The coffins inside, which were laying on top of elaborately crafted granite slabs, flew out onto the grass. "I was keeping him busy until you arrived," he called out to us, smiling. Lucius could have killed him in an instant, especially since Sergei had caught up to them long before we did.

"Good work," Aiden replied.

"Christian was the one who caught him. Give the praise to him, not me," Lucius told us. Mark, and ten other Divine Assassins joined us in the cemetery, and set up a wider perimeter around the outskirts in case any other vampires might be in the area.

Aiden and I walked over to Jack, who was being restrained by Sergei now. He was laying half in the grass, and half on top of the pieces of the cement tomb. "You've finally been caught, Jack. How does it feel? You didn't think it would ever happen, did you?"

Once again, he said nothing. His eyes were cutting into me though, and it gave me chills. He was a very terrifying man, not in looks, but in his actions. In fact, he was almost handsome. The evil inside him was what was so scary. He didn't use a lot of words, it was his cold, uncaring eyes that cut you to the core.

We heard a golf cart approaching in the distance, and figured it was a groundskeeper coming to see what the noises were. Christian was on top of it, darting away before the man could see what was happening.

"Did you know that your good friend, Elizabeth is living here in this very same town?" That got a small reaction out of him, as he raised his eyebrows ever so slightly in shock. "Maybe we should drop you off at her doorstep. After what you did to her, I am sure she'd love to see you again," I teased him.

I let him fester on the fact that she was still alive for a moment. Arabella came running up finally. "You got the asshole!" she exclaimed in joy. She wasted no time in walking right up to him, and kicking him in the face. I watched blood spray out of Jack's mouth from the impact as his head cocked to the side. She continued to kick him over and over, letting out her frustrations. It only took one quick instant for him to exploit her carelessness.

In her rage, Arabella knocked into Sergei, who, for a split-second let go of Jack. He took the opportunity to jump up and dart away. But he was disoriented, and didn't take off as fast as he would have liked. Sergei, Lucius, and I were all on top of it though. Sergei lit up his hands, and flung a fireball at him. It caught Jack's clothing on fire, and he began to flail his arms around trying to put it out, which slowed his fleeing down.

I snapped my fingers, and the darkness of the cemetery lit up with the magical ball of sunlight I had summoned. I wasted no time at all in launching it towards him. "Close your eyes!" I yelled out to my friends. We could all tell the moment it collided with Jack, and gave it a few seconds before opening our eyes again.

We ran up to the place he was standing in, and saw a pile of ashes. And that was the end of Jack the Ripper. The murders would stop, and the people in New Orleans would be much safer because of his death. Arabella was a mixture of feelings. She was excited that he was finally dead, but shaken up because of having to interact with him again. I put my arm around her and reassured her. "You'll never have to see him again, Arabella. You can finally stop worrying."

"I am so glad he is dead!" she sighed in relief.

"We all are!" Fiona replied.

My phone rang in my back pocket, and I picked it up. Mark was on the other end. "We have a situation here. On the east side of the cemetery," was all he said before he hung up.

"Let's go!" Aiden shouted, as he took off towards Mark and the Divine Assassins. When we got there, I could see that the men had already taken out several vampires. But they were surrounded by at least a dozen more.

A man, who we could clearly tell was the leader by his stance at the front of the vampires, stepped closer to us. "What is happening here?" he asked, with a slight French accent. When his eyes found me, he spoke again. "Identify yourself, woman. What Coven are you with?" he demanded of me.

"We are not part of any Coven. See this?" I said, as I snapped my fingers to summon my magic. "You're done asking the questions."

"You are the one who killed Misha and Lara!" the man wailed out. I put two and two together, and figured that this was their father, and the leader of their Coven. He was a man who looked to be in his fifties, salt and pepper hair, with a beard.

I smiled at him as I played with the magical ball in my hands. "The one and only."

"I am Ancil, and leader of my Coven. We are allied with one of the most powerful vampire leaders on this planet. You will pay for what you have done," he said, trying to threaten me.

"I gave your daughter a chance to try and convince you that you picked the wrong team. I didn't kill Misha on purpose. They attacked me first. We did, however, kill Lara on purpose. Bathory isn't the strongest vampire on the planet. Have you seen what I can do? I killed her once, and I will kill her again,"

He was confused, but stood his ground. "We have been allied with Bathory for some time now. I know what she can do. You are a fool," he scoffed at me.

"I warned you," I laughed, and launched my magical ball at one of his men. We all closed our eyes well in advance, knowing that the blinding light was coming. Mark, and the Divine Assassins had never seen me use my magic in person before.

"God Damn! That's bright!" he yelled out.

Once again, as I did with Claude and his men when they thought they had the upper hand, I went around to Ancil's group of vampires and began to touch them. "Stop!" he yelled out.

"If you tell me what I want to know, I will let you, and the remaining vampires live."

The vampires with me were running serious security, making sure that no other enemies were about to ambush us. "You're lying!" he spat out at me, still covering his face from the bright light that had blinded him temporarily.

He was right, I was lying, but he didn't need to know that. "No, actually, I'm not lying. Unlike all of you, with your backstabbing and murderous covens, we keep our word. I just need to know where Bathory is, and how many she has with her. Then, we'll be on our way. You don't mess with us; we won't mess with you."

One of his vampires, who spoke in French, told him not to do it. Ancil didn't take his advice. "She is residing in a mansion outside of town. Her dark fae are with her, at least one hundred of them. The Covens and vampires come and go. There are always dozens of vampires staying in the mansion."

The vampire started yelling at Ancil. "Don't tell them anything, you fool! If we tell her where Bathory is, Bathory will kill us. If we don't, she will kill us. We are dead either way!"

"Shut up!" he yelled back to the man in French again.

Not realizing that I could understand, and speak French...thanks to my learning potions from the Divine Assassins...I replied to him. "I said I would let you go if you cooperate. Give me the location, and you're free to go."

Ancil hesitated for a few moments, then began to tell me the location of Bathory's mansion. The other vampire was on him in an instant, attacking him. I walked over to the men, and put my hand on the man attacking Ancil, thinking that it would get him off of him. Instead, the magic incinerated both of them, because they were touching one another.

"Well, shit," I said. The remaining vampires in his coven began to flee, and I snapped my fingers once more to summon my sunlight. Lucius and Sergei were covering them in flames, and I shot three rounds of magic at them. The encounter was finally over.

"We need to get out of here right now. I can hear sirens in the distance. All the light surely attracted attention to the area," Christian commented.

"You're right, let's go," I said, as my vampires, and the Divine Assassins began to retreat. We had to get our cars out of the cemetery too, and we had to go slower than usual because of Arabella and the Divine Assassins. I hoped to God that they didn't have surveillance cameras set up. Thinking that it might be a good idea to check, I shouted out to Lucius asking if he would mind staying behind to scout it out.

"You got it. Was going to suggest that anyway," he replied, and took off into the night.

Aiden drove us back to the rental house. Christian and Fiona were with us, and they knew I was frustrated. "We had a major victory tonight, Skyy. Cheer up. At least we know the area that the mansion is in, we can find it with the help of the Divine Assassins technology," Christian said, trying to cheer me up.

"I know, Christian. We finally got Jack, I am beyond thrilled about that, but the encounter with Ancil really could have gone better."

"You weren't seriously considering letting them live, were you?" he asked me.

"Hell no! It's far too dangerous. I already know his alliance is with Bathory. I am not sure how she has convinced so many of these local vampires to join up with her, but we need to get to her as soon as we can, before she gains more strength and allies. Once we get home, I will go with Ridley to the Divine Assassins headquarters and start trying to locate the area that mansion might be in."

Aiden drove us back to the rental, and I told Ridley everything that had happened right away. He was thrilled to see Jack the Ripper was officially dead. He told Aimee that he would be back as soon as possible, and she was happy to stay behind with her new vampire girlfriends.

I kissed Aiden goodbye, and opened a portal to headquarters.

# Chapter 13

We had no issues locating the mansion. There wasn't much out that way, and it showed up clearly on satellite images. Now that we knew where she was, we needed to figure out the real plan. I had already thought about bringing in our Radiant fae friend, Dreamer, and getting her input. She had given me a pink crystal that I could use to summon her at any time back when we first met. I never abused it, and sometimes she would come into our dimension just to check in and say hello anyway. I felt like this was a good enough reason to call on her.

I wore the crystal around my neck most of the time, and if I didn't have it around my neck, it was in my pocket. You never know when you might need a fae's help. All I had to do was rub it, and she'd know my location right away. Letting the others know my plan first, I gently rubbed the crystal. It lit up softly, and before long I could see Dreamer's pink light glowing outside the window in the living room. I pointed to the front door, to let her know I'd let her in there.

Once she was safely in the house, she transformed from her tiny light-form, into her small humanoid form. Just as adorable as ever, Dreamer waved hi to everyone, and gave each of us a sweet hug. Aimee's face was worth a million dollars. She couldn't believe there was a fairy in front of her.

Dreamer fluffed her rose-colored hair, and straightened her very skimpy shirt before asking me, "What's going on Skyy? Is everything okay?"

"I've got some great news, actually. We just killed Jack the Ripper tonight! And…we got the location to the hideout that Bathory is in," I explained.

She clapped her tiny hands together and squealed. "Really!? I can't believe it! That is GREAT news indeed!"

"The reason I asked you here, is because I don't know how to take the next step. After doing some research, it looks like Bathory will just keep getting reincarnated from her phylacteries if she is killed here in our dimension. I can't think of a way to get her somewhere else, other than The Gloom, and there she will be surrounded by her dark fae allies."

"Hmm. Good point. Do you know how many dark fae she has with her at the hideout?" she asked.

"From a semi-unreliable source, we were told about one hundred. But I don't know how much of that is true, or even *if* this mansion is actually where she is located."

"None of you have scouted the area as of yet?"

"No, we just found the information out not too long ago, and had to do some digging to find out the exact location."

"Why don't you let me, and some of my friends scout for you? They will not be excepting us. We can fly in the area and go generally unnoticed during the day. The dark fae will all be inside, hiding from the sun," she suggested.

I looked at the others in the room for their opinions, and they all seemed to agree that it was a good plan. "Sounds like we have a plan, Dreamer. What are your thoughts, once you know the numbers?" I asked.

"I really have no idea as of yet! But we'll try to think of something!" she said cheerfully, as she opened up her beautiful wings, and popped back into her tiny light-form. I opened the door for her and watched her zip away into the slowly approaching dawn.

• • •

Rex was being summoned by Bathory once more. "What an impatient hag!" he mumbled to himself. He was sure that she would want to know if he had talked to the Elder fae about the magic that the girl who killed her was wielding. He asked them, and they had no clue. He was searching for the girl on his own, with no luck. Rex hated coming into this dimension, but would suffer it in order to get rid of Bathory. He had no idea how the phylacteries worked though, and that all of his hard work would be for nothing even if he did find Skyy.

The moment he walked through the tear into Bathory's dimension, he felt a jolt. Like he had been hit in the gut, he bent over and grabbed at his stomach. He had not felt anything that strongly in millennia. His skin began to crawl, and he looked down at his tattooed arms in shock. The magic on them was no longer glowing blue, but instead it was turning pink.

Valentina met him shortly after his arrival, and was also shocked to see his tattoos. "What is going on?" she said, as she pointed at them.

"Your guess is as good as mine," Rex replied, still looking over his arms.

"I can tell Bathory you are not feeling well, Rex. You need to find out what is happening," Valentina offered kindly.

"No, I will be fine. Let's see Elizabeth." Rex flew slowly through the dark, empty mansion. With the exception of the room Elizabeth stayed in, there wasn't much in the way of furnishings. All of the large windows were sealed up, or had thick curtains on them, which was fine with Rex. He couldn't be in the light for more than a few moments himself. He knocked on her door, and she called for him to enter.

Valentina was right behind him, and Elizabeth told her to go away. Rex looked back at her, and smirked. She knew full well of Rex's plans to get rid of her, and smiled back at him. Tolerating her for the time being, Valentina closed the door behind her and flew back downstairs.

"You don't look well, Rex. What is happening to your skin?" Bathory asked, from her bed. Naked as usual, she actually looked slightly better than the last time he had seen her.

"I...I don't know...I feel very odd," Rex replied, as he felt the jolt again. He remembered feeling this way so very long ago when he was torn from his sister.

Rex flew over to the window, and pulled the heavy curtain back to look outside. The sun blinded him for a moment; he wasn't used to bright light. "You idiot! Close the curtains immediately!" Bathory hollered out at him as she flung herself onto the floor to get out of the rays of sunlight that were streaming in the window.

"Oh my God," Rex whispered to himself.

"What!? What is it?!" Bathory exclaimed, wanting to know what was going on.

"It's…my sister!" he said in shock, before flying down the stairs of the mansion, leaving the curtain in Bathory's room wide open. Knowing she was left on her own, she crawled on the floor over to the window, and closed it herself, cursing him all the while.

"Valentina! Call the dark fae immediately. We must go outside! We are under attack!" he instructed her. She followed his orders without question, and within minutes they had a small army of dark fae waiting to go out into the sunlight.

"I will summon clouds to protect us, do not wander too far out from their protection or you will become very weak," Rex explained. Even in his weakened state, he was still one of the most powerful dark fae. He stepped out onto the front porch of the mansion, and conjured dark storm clouds in the sky above the house. The other fae joined him under their protective cover.

Dreamer felt the jolt too. As soon as she got close to the location, she fell from the sky to her knees in agony. The color on her wings changed from their usual rose-colored glow, to a deep plum color. She struggled through the jolts that kept knocking the wind out of her. As she got closer to the house, she spotted a face she had not seen in millennia; her brother, Rex. Now she knew why she was feeling the jolts.

She had a handful of Radiant fae with her, and ordered them to stand down, and not engage with the dark fae. They watched the army of dark fae flow out of the front door of the mansion. The sky got as black as night with storm clouds, and Rex flew out in front of the rest of the fae.

It brought tears to her eyes to see her brother, whom she had loved with all of her heart. He was her sworn enemy now, and this was the last thing she was expecting to see when she agreed to come out here and scout for Skyy.

Her tiny voice cracked with emotion, as she called out to Rex. "We are not here to fight, Rex, my dear brother!"

"Why else would you be here, sister?" he snarled to her.

"May we talk in private? The two of us?" she asked, knowing the answer would probably be no.

Rex thought about it for a moment, before agreeing. They were in a weakened state out in the sunlight, even with the cloud cover. Even though the Radiant fae were far fewer in numbers, he knew they could do serious damage to his dark fae in the day time. He nodded to his fae, and told them to retreat back into the house.

Dreamer asked her Radiant fae to do the same. They flew off into the woods, and waited patiently for her to call them back to her side. Rex flew over to her, and the clouds moved with him. She stared into his deep blue eyes that were so filled with hatred for her. "We need to talk, away from this house," she said to him.

The two of them flew off deep into the woods, several miles from the mansion, and away from Bathory's ears. "Why do you align yourselves with Bathory? She kills your people, and experiments on them!" Dreamer asked, confused about the situation.

"We gained much knowledge from her in the beginning. Father is the one who agreed to it, and we have no choice in the matter. He is quickly beginning to tire of her though," Rex replied openly, seeing this as an opportunity to possibly get their sworn enemies help on the matter. "I want her dead, once and for all."

Dreamer's mouth dropped open at his admission. She certainly wasn't expecting that. "As I am sure you know, we also want her dead. I am here because an ally of mine found her location. We were scouting the premises. Perhaps we can work together, this once?"

Rex could feel another jolt as he gazed at his sister. The powerful dark magic that had taken over his body and soul had a tight grip on him. He had always loved his sister; they were the best of friends. He never wanted to hurt her, and deep down inside he tucked away the love for her and protected it from the blackness that took over him. There was more at work here than he could control, but he agreed that working together to rid themselves of Bathory would be for the best.

Nodding at her once, she took that as a yes, and explained the situation. Rex could not believe his ears. The luck that he would meet up with her, at this very moment, was astonishing. "If we kill Bathory in another dimension, she will never be resurrected again," she told him, and went on to explain how the phylactery worked. He had *no* idea.

"She is after my friend, Skyy. If we can bait her somehow with Skyy, and get her into another dimension, we can kill her. How much power has she regained?" Dreamer asked of Bathory.

"Elizabeth is still very weak. Most days she cannot even get out of bed without help. However, if I let her drink from me, she has increased energy. Perhaps we can work out a plan," Rex replied, as he began to brainstorm.

"That is good news indeed." It killed Dreamer to see her brother this way. She wanted nothing more than to touch him, hug him, and tell him all the things that were happening back home in The Lucent.

They talked for a few more moments, and finally came up with a foolproof idea that would rid them of Bathory once and for all.

"I will let you know when my allies are ready, Brother," Dreamer said, as she took her leave.

Rex watched her flutter away, and couldn't believe the events that had just unfolded. His tattoos returned to their normal color once she was out of the area, and he felt much better. He hadn't seen Dreamer in so long, yet he could remember every detail as if it were yesterday.

Dreamer flew back to Skyy with a huge smile on her face. "You will never believe what just happened!" she exclaimed.

# Chapter 14

Listening to Dreamer tell me of her encounter with her dark fae brother gave me great hope that our vision could become a reality. But, being the skeptic that I am, I still had doubts. "This all sounds too good to be true. If we can actually pull it off, it would be amazing. But, the dark fae are our enemies, and even though Rex is your brother, we still have to tread carefully here."

"You are right, Skyy. The dark fae always have ulterior motives. I want to believe what he told me was true. His shock was as genuine as mine when he saw me. He seemed adamant on getting rid of Bathory for good. You have to remember, she has been torturing and experimenting on his kind for a long time now," Dreamer explained, with great enthusiasm. She wanted to believe it more than any of us.

"We will proceed, but with caution. Ridley and I will have to get the Divine Assassins together, and talk to them before we can put the entire plan into operation. I can't thank you enough for your help, Dreamer. As usual, you are a great friend, and your people always come through for us."

Dreamer and her friends took their leave shortly afterwards, and Ridley, Aiden, and I got ready to head over to the other rental house to fill in the Divine Assassins. As we were about to leave, my phone rang. It was Aimee's cousin, Pierce. Putting the phone to my ear as I slipped my shoes on, I greeted him. "Hello, Pierce."

Aimee told Pierce what had happened to her, and boy was he mad. But after seeing that we were taking great care of her, and keeping her safe, he lightened up. "I'm over at the club, and thought I should fill you in on what I heard last night. Word got out that the new vampire "coven" in town killed Ancil and some of his coven members. Apparently you didn't kill all of the vamps with him, some were on the way, heard the ruckus, and stopped a few blocks away. Good thing Ancil didn't live to find that one out, or he'd have killed them himself. None other than

Claude himself has taken over leadership of what is left of his coven. They are out for blood now, and are pulling together allies from other covens, even some of the ones they have sworn war against. It's ugly, Skyy. He's got people everywhere, not just in the French Quarter, looking for your gang."

Aiden heard every word, and sighed loudly. "Great, just what we need right now."

"That little turd Claude wants me, then he'll get me. And I'll give him what I gave Ancil. They can bring all the covens together, and I will do away with the whole lot of them at once," I said, angrily.

"Just thought I'd let you know; they will be scouring the streets looking for you. I hope you're right, a few dozen less vamps here in New Orleans sound good to me," he chuckled.

"Claude must be a special kind of stupid, to want to mess with me after seeing what I can do now. But that's okay, makes it easier to kill him."

"Well, you just let me know if you need a location to take care of business. I own a few warehouses in the area, one of which is currently empty. Perfect place for mass vampire genocide," Pierce said.

"Oh, really?" I questioned him, my curiosity piqued.

"Mmm hmm. Just outside of the French Quarter too. If you can funnel them in there, it's all yours. I will text you the address. If one of you can swing by the club before it gets dark, I'll give ya the keys."

"Pierce, we can't thank you enough, but just know there is a good chance we'll damage, or destroy, the building. We can pay you in full, and then some, for the damages though," I told him, visualizing the building after I would be done with it.

"As long as it can help you guys, it's no big deal. We'll work out payments and such if the time comes."

"Thank you so much. I'll send one of my friends down there to get the keys right away. Let me know if anything else arises. Chances are, we'll try to get over there tonight and see what kind of trouble we can cause."

Christian was walking into the room as I hung up, and offered to go get the keys for me. "You sure you don't mind?" I asked him.

"Nah, it's a nice day out. Won't take that long to get there and back," he said, as he put his own shoes on.

"Thanks," I told him as the three of us walked out the door. He hopped into one of our rental cars, and blasted some music as he pulled out of the driveway. Aiden and I walked over to the Divine Assassins rental house hand in hand.

Luckily, we caught my grandpa there. His white hair was perfectly combed for once, and he was eating a slice of pizza as he was going over paperwork that was spread out on a table. "Hello, Skyy! Would you like some pizza?" he said, as he slid the box over my way, before remembering that I no longer ate human food. "Oh, sorry. Habit," he chuckled kindly.

I laughed with him, as Aiden went to shake his hand in greeting. "Did the men fill you in on the events from last night?" I asked.

With a mouthful of pizza, he nodded at me. He wiped his mouth off, and swallowed before answering. "Yes! Good work from all of you. Sorry I wasn't there to see the bastard die."

"It was really exhilarating. But now we have all the Covens here looking for us. I came over here to tell you that we spoke to the Radiant fae, and have been devising a plan for Bathory, but now I think that may need to go on hold until we can take care of these covens, and the vampire Claude who is leading the charge."

Grandpa wiped his hands off on his red Hawaiian shirt, and stood up from the table. "Have you thought of any kind of plans for that yet?"

Aiden chimed in, "The girl who we are protecting, Aimee...her cousin owns a large warehouse that isn't in use. He gave us access to that. Could the Divine Assassins help us set things up there for an ambush?"

"Of course. How many vampires are we talking?"

"I don't know. A lot. There are so many covens here, I have lost count. But Claude has apparently united at least a few people from them to help fight for his cause. Apparently we are the biggest threat to ever hit this town," I joked, as I flexed my arms and laughed.

Aiden touched my muscle and pretended to be impressed. "Nice. You work out often?"

The three of us laughed together, before continuing on with our plans. "We can go to the building as soon as you get access to it. If this is something you're wanting to set up tonight, I can have about sixty men ready within a few hours. If you need more than that, we'll need more time. I want to see what the area, and structure look like before we set up though," Grandpa told me.

"Of course. Christian went to get the keys to the place, we can have them to you within an hour. As for Dreamer, and the plans to move ahead with Bathory..."

I filled Grandpa in on the entirety of what was discussed with the Radiant fae. He was also skeptical, just like I was. We decided that there would need to be more safety measures in place before he was comfortable letting me go forward with the plan. He would work on things, while we hopefully took care of Claude and his crew.

Christian had the keys from Pierce in no time, and I asked him to drop them off over at the Divine Assassins rental house. We took our leave after that, and let them get to work doing surveillance on the warehouse. We heard back from Grandpa fairly fast. He thought the building would work out just fine, and had already put some of the men to work moving weapons and supplies over there.

"It's not going to be hard at all to lure them in there, if they have that many men out on the streets looking for us. I have a sneaking suspicion Claude won't ask Bathory for that private meeting because his own revenge is clouding his vision. Which is both good, and bad, right now. One bad guy at a time, I suppose," I said, as I pondered how this would all turn out.

Lucius, Christian, and Aiden were trying to decide how to work things out. We needed someone to bait them into the warehouse, and since the most likely place they would be looking for us would be the French Quarter, we'd have to have someone who could get out of there without getting caught. That left me out, since I couldn't levitate or teleport across short distances yet.

Christian was the first to volunteer, feeling proud of himself for catching Jack. "I'll do it!" he piped up, with a huge smile on his face.

Lucius returned his smile, but shot him down. "I appreciate your enthusiasm Christian, but I think either Sergei or I should be the one to bait. In the event we get overwhelmed, we can use our fire as defense."

Sergei had joined us shortly after we began the discussion, and nodded. In his thick Russian accent, he agreed with Lucius. "Yes. I will be the one. No problem."

"We will hide the other vampires in cars, and have some Divine Assassins drive them to the warehouse then, and wait for you to funnel them into the building. There will probably be many of them after you, Sergei, so be prepared," Aiden explained to him.

"Yes, I know. Hopefully, everything will go as planned," he assured us.

"All we have to do now is wait for the Divine Assassins to call us and let us know they are ready," I said.

We didn't have to wait too long. Just before sunset they called, and told us they were sending a few cars to transport us over there. Aimee and Arabella would stay behind, along with one Divine Assassin to make sure she didn't blood lust around Aimee.

Ridley was saying goodbye to Aimee once more, as we gathered up all the items we'd need for our ambush. I dressed light, as did Aiden. Some comfy black and pink workout pants, a cute matching racerback tank top, my tennis shoes, and my hair in a ponytail and I was all set. Aiden was wearing slim fit designer jeans, and a black t-shirt. He could wear just about anything and manage to look drop-dead gorgeous.

Aimee was crying, and we could tell she was embarrassed, so they went back to his bedroom for a moment. "It'll be fine; the Divine Assassins do this for a living. We have got everything covered," he assured her.

Sniffling, she replied. "I know, Ridley. I am just so scared, being dropped into this brand new world I have no idea about. What if all of you got killed, and nobody came back? What would I do?"

Apparently she greatly underestimated us, but I suppose it *could* happen. "Aimee, trust me. There is little, to no chance that all of us would get killed. The Divine Assassins have magical abilities, and weapons, that even your wildest dreams couldn't imagine. The vampires are all way more powerful than most of the other vamps we will be fighting. And with Skyy's new recent magical powers, there is no chance for them. I promise you, we will all come back just fine," he said honestly.

I could tell he had embraced her into a hug, because her sniffles became muffled for a moment. "This will all be over soon, and I'll be back before you know it," he whispered, as he kissed her.

"Let's go, Ridley!" Lucius shouted out. They emerged from the room shortly after that. Grandpa had sent the man over to watch Arabella and Aimee, so we were good to go.

We piled into the rental cars, laying down in the backseats so we wouldn't be spotted if we drove by any vampires on the lookout. It took more cars because of that, but better safe, than sorry.

The ride to the warehouse was fairly short, and I didn't mind being pushed up against Aiden in the backseat. His cologne and soap scent was always a pleasure to take in. Once we parked, he kissed me on the lips and told me that he loved me.

We quickly filed into the warehouse, and took our positions. Grandpa was there, perched up in the rafters no less. They wanted me up on the second floor that overlooked the lower level. Nobody else besides Aiden was near me, and he would have to move away in the event I summoned huge amounts of my sunlight. I had charged up for a few minutes earlier in the day, and was good to go.

We waited, and waited for Sergei to call, but he didn't. He had been out in the French Quarter for over an hour, there was no way someone...whether they were looking for him or not...wouldn't have spotted him by now. I told Lucius to call him, to find out what was going on.

I heard them talking, Sergei was fine and unharmed. He was wandering around the French Quarter, popping in and out of every vampire bar he could find. There were plenty of vampires, but none of them seemed to care about him. I could tell Lucius was puzzled, and so was I.

Moments later, Sergei called back and said that he had spotted Claude in a vampire bar. "He recognized me, grinned at me, but neither he nor his men engaged me. What shall we do?" he asked.

Just as he said that, we heard several feet approaching outside the warehouse. "Outside!" several of us shouted at the same time. Before anyone could even react, we heard multiple things happening. They were throwing Molotov cocktails at the entire building, and had tossed in grenades after a small bomb was launched through the front area of the warehouse. It happened so fast, we were caught off guard.

The Divine Assassins by the front door were all laying on the floor, covered in blood. I could see about ten of them down there, but the smoke was so thick, and getting thicker from the fires that had erupted, that I couldn't tell if they were alive or not. The rest of us were running down from the areas we had been staked out in. Fire was quickly consuming the building, and we had to get out. As I ran down to the lower level, I snapped my fingers, getting my magical sunlight ready.

There were three vampires that were outside, and Divine Assassins had quickly disabled them. They had been silvered, and were paralyzed. "What do you want to do with them?" one of the men, named Charlie, asked both me, and Grandpa.

"We already know who they were sent by. Claude doesn't value their lives, or he wouldn't have sent them here," I said, as I walked over to each one of them and turned them to ash with a touch of my hand.

The vampires were working quickly to drag out the bodies of the men who were injured before the warehouse went up in flames. "We have to get out of here immediately. Cops will be here any minute," Aiden said as he looked at my grandpa.

"We can open portals. Men! If you can open a portal back to headquarters, do it! Grab one of the injured, and get them out of here now!" he shouted out. The Divine Assassins took action quickly, and did as they were told. "The rest of you, get the vamps out of here and back to the rental!" he added on.

Ridley and I opened our portals right away, and each grabbed a vampire. I took Christian, he took Lucius.

We appeared back in our rental house, as other portals opened around us bringing in the rest of my vampire friends. Ridley and I gasped out loud when we looked around. "Oh my God!" I whispered as I put my hand to my mouth.

The front door to the house had been kicked in. The Divine Assassin who was put on watch, was laying on the living room floor, dead. He had been shot in the head, and fresh blood was all around him. I started to feel that irresistible urge to feed upon smelling it, but had to fight it. Aiden rushed to my side after he was portaled in by another Divine Assassin, to make sure I was okay from the warehouse incident.

Ridley was frantically looking for Aimee. "Aimee!" he was screaming out over and over, as he ran to each room.

"Arabella is missing as well," Fiona informed me, after she swept all the rooms.

Ridley's phone began to ring. I snatched it out of his hand so fast, he didn't even know what had happened. I knew who it would be. "You mother fucker," I said to Claude.

"Hello, Skyy. As I am sure you have gathered, we have two of your friends here with us," he sneered on the other end.

"We need to get out of this house, right now! They could be waiting to attack once more," Lucius whispered out to the room.

The Divine Assassins once more began to open up portals, and shuffled the vampires out of the house. Ridley, Aiden, and I were all that was left as I continued my conversation with Claude. "Your idiot friend who went to the French Quarter earlier to meet with the human led us right to you. Didn't think we had humans working for us, did you?" he said again, egging me on.

"Claude. What is it that you want?" I got right to the point.

"I want you, Skyy. Your boyfriend wouldn't hurt either. And eye for an eye type thing. Bathory and I both want the same thing it seems: your head on a platter."

Aiden was gesturing that we needed to follow the others, and get out of the house. He was right, and I knew nothing I said to Claude at that moment would matter, so I hung up the phone, and almost snapped it in half with anger. "To the castle," I said to Ridley. He nodded, and opened a portal for himself and was gone in an instant. I took Aiden through my own portal. We appeared in Scotland, in Aiden's castle. I had no idea where the others had gone, but as long as they were safe that was all that mattered. We could all regroup in a bit.

Ridley was so shaken up, that he was about to faint. "Sit down, friend," Aiden said, as he slid a chair over to him. He immediately plopped down and put his head in his hands.

"Aimee got taken. Again! I don't know that we'll be able to get her out alive a second time. She was so scared to be left alone, and I promised her everything would be fine!" he wailed out.

My anger was rising more and more by the second. I needed blood, and badly. I made a gesture to Aiden that I was drinking out of a cup, and he disappeared to get some for me. I paced the castle floors back and forth until he returned, letting Ridley talk to himself.

I chugged my mug of blood down in two gulps, and it made me feel slightly better. "We are so stupid. I never even thought that they would have humans looking for us during the day. Why did it never cross our minds?!" I yelled out.

"They must have sent in humans to capture them, because the house was warded. No vampire could have entered there. We underestimated Claude greatly. Now poor Arabella and Aimee pay the price," Aiden theorized.

"That is the only logical thing. So, now what?" I replied.

Ridley was taking deep breaths in, and out, to calm down. His hair was a frazzled mess from running his hands frantically through it. "She will never forgive me for this. I told her she was safe," he said again.

I went over to him and placed my hand on his back, rubbing it softly. "Yes, she will. She loves you," I assured him.

His head popped up from his hands, and he looked at me in awe. "You think she loves me?"

Aiden smiled at him, and nodded. "If I was a betting man, I'd put all my money on yes. I have seen the way she looks at you."

This gave Ridley hope. He smiled, and blushed. If the poor girl made it out alive, I was pretty sure she'd forgive him as well. "We have to call the others, and meet up right away," Ridley said. I tossed him his phone, and he called Mark.

They were in another house the Divine Assassins kept for occasions such as this, in Arizona. Mark gave the phone to my grandfather, and Ridley handed his phone to me.

"So what is it that they want, Skyy? We will need to reform our plan," he said from the other end. I could tell he was shaken up as well.

"They want me. Plain and simple. Claude seems to be on a rampage, he wants me dead, and Aiden for good measure. I killed his wife, his sister-in-law, and his father-in-law. Plus, pretty much his whole Coven. He is working outside of Bathory's orders, no doubt. She would never have him out on the streets acting this reckless."

"We have no idea where he may be hiding the girls?" he asked.

"I sure don't. I don't know that anyone else would either. We have all been sticking together closely."

"Let us all portal over to your location, so we can discuss. You're at the castle?"

"Yes."

The phone clicked off, and portals began to open on the grounds. Before long, Mark, my grandfather, my vampire family, and a few of the Divine Assassins were at the castle. "How are the men who were injured in the explosion? Any word?" I asked.

"One is dead. The others will recover," Grandpa said glumly.

"Shit! I can't believe this happened!" I yelled out again.

"Perhaps meeting with your Radiant fae friend would be a good next step. See what they think, perhaps they could find out something for us?" Grandpa suggested.

Ridley's phone rang again, and it was Claude. Of course, he wanted to speak to me. I grabbed the phone from him, and put it up to my ear. "I see you've left town. Smart move. Now, can we finish our conversation from earlier?"

"I'm listening."

"I'll hold your friends for no more than twenty-four hours before the torture begins. You, and the boyfriend, can surrender yourself to me before then, and I will let them go unharmed. You will let my men restrain you with silver, and we have a deal," he explained.

"Very well. Give me an address. We will meet you there before the twenty-four hours are up. I expect my friends to be untouched. That means no feeding."

Claude hung up, and the phone received a message shortly after with an address back in New Orleans. "You're right, we need to talk to Dreamer. We are working on borrowed time right now," I said, as I reached around my neck for the pink crystal. A few moments passed, and she showed up as expected.

Dreamer could tell right away that something was wrong. "Oh no, friends! What has happened?" she asked us, as she gave me a hug.

"We are in a predicament, that I am not sure how we can get out of. I need some advice, and probably your help again, Dreamer."

She smiled at me and nodded, as I offered her a seat. We filled her in on the events thus far, and she gasped when we told her about our ambush that got ambushed. "Claude gave us a location, but it's not Bathory's mansion. I fear he is working alone, and I have no idea what we might walk in to."

Dreamer thought on things for a moment, then stood up. "Well. I guess this is as good of a time as any to test the new formed, shaky alliance with the dark fae. I will see what information I can get from them. It'll be fast, since I know you're on a timer. Be back soon!"

With that she opened a portal right there in the castle, hopped through it, and was gone.

# Chapter 15

Dreamer gathered her closest friends, Holland, and Pacific, and took off to the mansion in New Orleans. She could tell Rex was not there, because her wings were not glowing. The painful jolt she felt last time was also missing. All they could do now was wait, since she had no other way of contacting him. Several hours had passed before she began to feel odd. Sure enough, her wings began to turn to a deep plum color, and her body was being wracked with the jolts.

Rex had entered the mansion, and immediately knew that his sister was nearby. He had come to talk to Valentina, but would surely have to see Bathory as well. Besides the jolts he felt from her presence, he was alerted that something was amiss from all the commotion in the normally quiet and lifeless mansion.

There were dozens of vampires there, and several of them were being tortured and held captive. He lifted up off the cold, tiled flooring, and flew to where the noise was coming from. What would have served as a dining room, was now holding captive vampires. He recognized one of them right away, as one of Bathory's closest allies. The bald one that was always lurking around. The dark fae, including Valentina, were observing, and standing guard.

He walked up next to her, and placed his hand gently on her lower back. Just that one simple gesture sent the dark fae Captain into overdrive, but she had to contain herself. Rex smiled down at her, and asked, "What is all of this about?"

Before Valentina could reply, Bathory…from her bedroom upstairs…heard Rex's entrance, and called out to him. "Rex! Come up here this instant darling!" He rolled his eyes at the sound of her voice. Valentina stifled a laugh.

"I'll be back," he told her, as he took to the air once more to fly up to the hag's room. He opened the door, and as usual, she was in her bed, naked. He glanced over to the corner where there were two metal dog crates. Inside of them was a human, and a vampire, both female. "What is this?" he said, pointing to the cages.

"My new pets," Elizabeth said, laughing manically. Rex just stared at her, waiting for the real answer. She waved her hand at him. "Okay, okay. They are my collateral. These are friends of Skyy's. We'll only need one left alive, and I am deciding which one I want to kill."

Not sure how all of this might interfere with the plan he had concocted with his sister earlier, he decided to try to get some more answers out of her. But he could tell she wanted his blood badly, and next would come the sex. He was right...seconds later she was patting the mattress for him to come sit down.

His tattoos were glowing pink, and he knew she would notice. He hadn't even sat down on the bed before she started removing his shirt. She was breathing deep and fast, already worked up at the sight of him. "How did you come across these women?" Rex asked, trying to prolong the inevitable. He could tell she had fed off of a human recently, her skin was more vibrant than usual, and she had more energy than most visits. And, for once, she wasn't covered in caked on, dried up blood. Her hair was clean and shiny, and she smelled like a normal being who took care of herself.

She got up on her knees and was kissing on his neck now, breathing and panting in his ear. "My idiot minion, Claude, thought he could trick me. He was going behind my back, plotting to kill Skyy on his own, even after I told him not to," she said, as she nipped at his neck gently, drawing blood. She moaned as she licked it with her tongue. "One of his men ratted him out, came to me and told me everything. We raided his place, and found these two there. Claude is being tortured now, until I can finish him off later."

Elizabeth's hands moved down over Rex's chest, and sure enough she asked him why his tattoos were glowing. "It is a lingering effect of being close to my sister. When they attacked the other day, we came too close to one another. It shall fade soon," he bluffed.

Rex was distracted looking at the women in the dog cages. The human was passed out, but still alive. The vampire was terrified. She was mouthing *"please help me!"* to him. Normally, he would not care what happened to a vampire. But since his sister was allied with this particular group, he would probably need to figure out a way to get them out of there. He nodded at her once, as Bathory suckled at his neck. She was straddling one of his legs while up on her knees, pleasuring herself. He flinched as she bit into his neck harder.

Pulling her off of him, he glared at her. Her normally black eyes were changing colors so rapidly that he couldn't keep up. It was not normal, and it always disturbed him when he saw it. "Not so hard, woman," he warned her. She laughed at him, and went back to his neck, not wanting to waste a drop of his magical blood. Once she was done at his neck, she pulled her fingers out of herself, and tried to place them in his mouth. He shook his head, and pushed her hand away. "No," he said, warning her again. There was only so much he would tolerate from her, and he was not about to taste her wetness.

"Very well. You're no fun anymore, Rex," she pouted, as she shoved him back onto her bed and straddled him. Taking his erect penis in her hand, she guided it into her soaking wet flower. Rex stared at the ceiling, wondering what his sister was doing here, and how he would get the women out of Bathory's room, as she rode his cock fast and hard. Even while preoccupied with thought, it still felt good, if he didn't look at her. He closed his eyes, and once again imagined a beautiful, dark fae in her place, and was surprised when it was Valentina's image that appeared. He smiled at the vision, and before long he had reached his climax. Elizabeth had yet to reach hers, and he tossed her off of him like a ragdoll.

She stood up off the floor where she had flown to, and glared at him. "What are you doing, imbecile?!" she shouted out.

Rex stood up, and grabbed her by her upper arms. "Be careful how you talk to me, vampire. My generosity of my blood to you is a favor. And your charm is quickly wearing out. I am not one of your servants who you can boss around at will. I am a

Prince. Remember that. I came here to see my Captain, so I am taking my leave."

Elizabeth stood before him, with her mouth hanging open at his statement. She rubbed her arms where his powerful hands had just been grasping her. He had never talked back to her before. A slow grin emerged on her face, as she found that she actually liked it.

Though she had just dined on the powerful, and magical blood of a dark fae Prince, she still craved more. Glancing over at the dog crates, she smiled at the women. The human would be her after-dinner dessert.

Rex flew back down to the lower level of the mansion, and found Valentina in the same location as before. "I need you to come with me," he said, as he took her one, and only, arm. Silently she nodded, and followed him out of the mansion to the grounds out front.

He transformed into his light-form, and she followed suit. They flew off into the night sky together, far away from the mansion. He could tell he was getting closer to his sister, because the jolts got stronger and stronger. Before long, he came to the same meeting place as last time, and saw his sisters familiar pink light in the distance. Valentina questioned him, "What is this?"

"Do you trust me, Valentina?" he asked her.

"With my life," was her immediate response.

"We have to do this, to help our people. To save ourselves."

She didn't speak another word, and followed his lead. All of the fae went into their humanoid forms once they met. "Dreamer," Rex said, acknowledging her.

"Hello, Rex," she returned happily. Hearing her cheerful voice cracked away at his hardened emotions. "We have some news, our friend Skyy was ambushed by one of Bathory's vampires. They took two of my friend's hostage. I am wondering if you have any information on the matter."

Rex nodded, and spoke. "I'm afraid it's worse than you think. The vampire that captured the women was ratted out. The rat went to Bathory, who had no idea one of her men was working against her wishes. They now have the women, and the rogue vampire is in custody. Elizabeth means to kill one of the women tonight," he informed them.

Dreamer put her tiny hands to her mouth. "Oh no! We have to stop that from happening. Are you sure they will keep the women at the mansion?"

"Yes, Bathory thinks she has a bargaining chip in the girls. She is too weak to move elsewhere, and her mansion is fully equipped to deal with the sun, and she has all the protection she needs. She won't move."

"We need to move forward with our plans sooner than expected then," Dreamer told him, as she pondered the terrible situation.

"I agree."

# Chapter 16

Dreamer returned to us within a few hours. This time, it was the look on her face, not ours, that scared me.

"I have some bad news. The girls were taken to Bathory's mansion. The vampire you're looking to meet up with for the trade, was ratted out by another vampire in her employ. He is now being held, along with your friends, in her mansion. But, I think we have a solid plan. We will need to act right away, as my brother told me Bathory means to kill one of them tonight," she said.

"Great. Well, it could be worse, I suppose. At least they are both in the same location now. Two birds, one stone," Christian laughed. We all agreed on that fact.

"So tell us what you've come up with, Dreamer," Aiden said.

"You all must know that this is going to be very dangerous. The plan we discussed earlier is still in motion, and will stay the same for the most part. My brother will make sure Bathory is in the state she needs to be in, but just entering the mansion in and of itself is a dangerous task," she warned us, with all seriousness.

"We know the risks. We have no choice but to take them. Our friend's lives, and the lives of countless victims she could take hostage, are all counting on us. We will need a few moments to gear up, gather supplies and whatnot. Where should we meet up?" I asked her.

"When we are ready, I will go first, and let Rex know. You will portal in right on the property," she replied. Nobody in the room spoke, but we all exchanged glances.

"And, you're *SURE* that you can trust your brother on this?" I questioned her once more on the matter.

"I would not be putting myself in harm's way if I didn't believe he was being truthful. One day, when this is all over, I will tell you our story."

That was all I needed to hear. If she was willing to lay her life down for this, then that was all the convincing I needed. She wouldn't be leading us into a trap.

"Okay then. If you trust him, I trust in you. We will be ready on your notice," I told her, as we began to spring into action. "And I look forward to hearing your story, too."

Dreamer smiled, and left us to gear up. She would notify me via the pink crystal of hers that I carried that the coast was clear.

Ridley was a nervous wreck. "If Bathory has her, who knows what shape she will be in!" he exclaimed, about to lose his composure.

"Ridley, we'll get through this. Last we heard, she was alive. Even if she sustains injuries, there are ways we can heal her. Let's focus on the task at hand. I need you with me, and at full strength," I encouraged him.

"I'll be right there at your side, Skyy. We'll beat this once and for all," he said, as he stood up with confidence.

Aiden and I went to our room in the castle to change clothes. My sword was back in New Orleans at the rental house, which was hopefully still standing. I doubted that the sword would be destroyed in a fire, but it would be nice to keep it in one piece. For now, good old fashioned magic, and my new sunlight powers were all that I'd be bringing with me. Aiden closed the door, and came to embrace me right away.

"This scares the shit out of me, Skyy. You know I'd normally tell you to sit this one out, but I know you're the strongest among us right now. I can't even get near you when you're using the magic," he said, as he took my face into his hands.

I had been so wrapped up in all the events that seemed to keep happening one after the other, that I really didn't stop to think about how dangerous all of this actually was. "I know. When I step back from all of this, and really think about it, it's crazy. But we have to do this, there is no other option," I told him, as I looked into his green eyes that were filled with worry.

"I wish there was. I would give anything just to keep you safe. But once this is all over, maybe we can go back to a semi-normal life. Whatever that may be..." he let the sentence drift off.

I chuckled, and reminded him who he was married to. "A normal life is probably out of the question. But another nice vacation might be needed."

Aiden kissed me deeply, and smiled. "Yes. Another vacation sounds splendid."

A moment of panic swept over me, as I thought about my mom and dad, and my cousin Cate back home. What if I didn't make it out alive? Who would tell them? What would they even say? Letting out a long breath of air I hadn't realized I was holding, I fell to my knees. Aiden moved down with me, still holding on.

Tears began to flow from my eyes. "I used to look for adventure, and ghosts all the time in my mortal life. Now, here I am, wrapped up in the craziest scenario I could ever imagine, and all I want to do is hug my mom and dad right now. To go back to our little life we had in Massachusetts. I want Cupcake snuggling at our feet at night as we crawl into bed in the awesome bedroom at the mansion back there. To be the maid-of-honor in Cate's wedding. You worry about me, all the time, and I hate doing this to you," I sobbed out, planting my face into his shoulder.

"Skyy...Skyy...shhh. Milady, it will be alright. We always get through things, one step at a time. You beat Bathory once, we will beat her again. Once it's all over, we can go back to Massachusetts if that is what you desire," he said, as he comforted me.

"I hate putting you through this. The thought of my parents getting a phone call that I am dead, and not even knowing the whole truth of it kills me. They don't even know Grandpa is alive!"

"You had no choice in your lineage. Your ancestor put all of this in motion centuries ago. The war with Bathory, Grandpa becoming part of the Divine Assassins. All of it was out of your control. This would have happened whether you had met me, or not. And I am glad it happened afterwards, because I feel like I have played some part in keeping you alive," he said, as he smiled at me.

"Yes, of course you have, Aiden. I thank my lucky stars every single day that I met you. In more ways than one, you have saved me. But I hate lying to my parents. All of this, from the day I met you in that cemetery, has happened so fast I have not had time to step back and look at all of it," I replied.

"I know it seems hard right now, but this is the life that we live. Normal vampires don't form relationships with humans, because their life is gone in the blink of an eye. Most of them treat humans as only a food source. Those that fall in love, either turn them, or die from a broken heart. Both you, and Arabella are struggling to let go of your human lives. It is hard to come to terms with, but eventually you will have to break off contact with your parents. Or tell them the truth," Aiden told me, with sympathy and love in his eyes. It was nothing that I had not heard before.

I understood why he hesitated so much about turning me now. Wiping my tears away, I hugged him tightly. "I love you, Aiden Carrick. Thank you so much for loving me, and believing in me."

He smiled at me, and replied, "I love you too, Skyy Carrick." We embraced for several moments before I let him go.

"Now, let's go kick some vampire ass," I said, wiping the remaining tears off of my face and standing up. My meltdown would have to wait for a more convenient time. We suited up in a flash, both wearing our black combat pants, and tight fitting black t-shirts. All we needed them to say on the back was "Mr. & Mrs. Carrick" for it to be complete.

Once I saw that all of my vampire friends and Divine Assassins were ready, we signaled Dreamer through the pink crystal. All we could do now was wait.

$$\cdots$$

Elizabeth had called the vampire who told on Claude up to her quarters. His name was Jared, and he was a fairly newly made vampire. His eyes were light blue, and his hair was a dirty blonde color. He was a younger man when he was turned, possibly in his early twenties. She would reward his loyalty by letting him serve her. With nervous hands, he opened the doors to her living quarters. Rarely did she ever leave them, and none of the vampires got the pleasure of seeing her up close like this.

Jared glanced over to the corner where the two women were being held right away. Then his eyes went back onto Bathory, who was sitting on the edge of her massive bed, playing with her ebony hair. "You called for me?"

"That one there, the human. She will be my entertainment for tonight. I know since Claude is...no longer...in my service, that you have no idea what I expect from you. See that box over by the tub? Go fetch it," she ordered to him, frustrated that she had to train another minion. Claude had served her so well, for so long.

Jared did as she asked and retrieved the box. "Put it up on that table there, by the tub," she instructed. "Now open it. Inside you will find numerous tools. You may have no idea what some of them do, but you will learn in time what it is that I need. Some of my favorites we use quite often, and some of them are reserved for special occasions."

Jared looked through the box of horrors. Even though he drank from humans, he could not imagine an instance where any of these torture devices could be used. He had heard rumors, and legends about Elizabeth Bathory. But being in front of her now, staring down at these tools made him queasy. He wasn't sure he could fill the role that Claude did for her.

She could see the fear in his eyes. Claude was the same way, in the beginning. She had to build him up, mold him into what she needed him to be. Perhaps she gave him too much leeway. This one, her new pet, would be kept on a tight leash. "Well! Don't just stand there like an idiot! I thirst! Bring the human out of the cage, and put her into the tub. Her clothes must be stripped off first," she barked out, as she clapped her hands at him like a mother to a child.

Looking away from the tools, he nodded at her, and got the courage to go over to the dog crates that held two women. One was a vampire, but the other one…she smelled lovely to him. She was a human, and he wanted to taste her sweet blood more than anything. Maybe if he did a good job, Bathory would share. He yanked open the door to the crate, and grabbed her by the hair. The vampire in the crate next to her screamed out, "NO! You asshole! Let her go! Take me instead!"

Jared looked over to Elizabeth to see her reaction. She dismissed the vampire girl with the flick of her wrist. "Carry on with the plan, pay no attention to her," she said, nonchalantly.

The human was weak, and barely conscious. "Feed her a few drops of blood, to heal her. But no more than that," Bathory told him.

He did as he was told, and bit into his wrist to feed the human his blood. It healed her in moments, and she was coherent enough to know what was happening now. She struggled against his strong body, to no avail. Looking over at Bathory, she shouted out, "You cunt! You have no idea what is coming your way! Kill me, go ahead! It won't do anything but make them even madder!"

Bathory got up off of her bed, still energized by the blood of the dark fae Prince from earlier. She smiled wickedly at the girl as she moved towards her. "Put her in the tub, Jared."

The new minion did as she asked, and put the now-naked girl into the tub. She fought him the entire way. Little did he know that this was how Bathory liked her girls. He figured that she would just want the blood. But he was quickly seeing that she enjoyed the hunt, just as much as the feast.

Bathory crawled into the tub, as the girl stood before her at the foot of it. The young woman was trembling in fear, trying to cover her private parts as best she could. "So what is it, exactly, that Skyy and the vampires find so special about you?" she asked, glaring at the girl trying to figure it out.

The vampire in the cage had not stopped screaming since Jared had removed the human. Without even casting a glance towards her, Bathory held one of her hands outside of the tub.

"You *will* shut up, now," she ordered. In an instant, the vampire girl stopped her yelling. Jared tensed up at the show of Bathory's power.

Bathory glanced at the girls pierced nipples, and pierced clitoris. "So what is the purpose of that? Does it actually feel good, or is it just to be in style?" she said, as she waved her hand around in front of the girl's private parts.

With no reply, the girl just glared at her, trembling. "Answer me!" Elizabeth screamed out, as she sat up from her relaxed position in the tub, and ripped one of the nipple rings right off of the girl's body. She yelled out in agony, but did not answer her. Bathory's eyes narrowed, and she smiled at the sight of the blood dripping down from the girl's breast. She noticed that the girl did not fuss for long, so she took her finger and rubbed it in the blood that was flowing. Putting it to her mouth, she closed her eyes in bliss, savoring the taste. It certainly was no dark elf Prince blood, but knowing that this was an ally of Skyy's made the occasion something extra special.

In one fast swipe of the hand, she ripped the other nipple ring out. Again, a short scream from the girl was all that she got. Her eyes were closed now, as she convulsed in pain. But she did not give Bathory the pleasure of seeing her plead or beg. Elizabeth got onto her knees for the second time that night, and placed her mouth onto one of the bleeding breasts. Moaning as she suckled on it, she shoved her fingers into the open wound of the other one. The pain made the girl falter, and fall to her knees. That was what she wanted to see. Removing her bloodied lips from the girl's body, she laughed.

"Jared!" she shouted out, scaring the young apprentice into action. "See that chain there? Our young lady likes pain, and we shall give it to her. Pull it, and grab the device from the ceiling," she said as she leaned back in the tub, still licking her fingers. Jared pulled the hook device down from the ceiling, and Bathory barked out orders to him on how to use it properly.

"We'll just start with her shoulder area first. Those hooks there…put them into her," she explained, pointing at the blood-encrusted, rusty hooks.

Jared was not at all comfortable doing this, but he knew he had no choice. He would do it, or she would kill him too. He grasped the girl's shoulders as gently as he could, silently apologizing to her. One of his special abilities was being able to project his thoughts into a human mind. He knew she could hear him, but also knew that it didn't matter much at this point. Taking the first rusted hook into his shaking hands, he punctured her skin just over her shoulder blades. It made a terrifying "*pop!*" sound, and he cringed.

"Oh! Come now, Jared! This is the best part. Don't be a baby!" Elizabeth teased, as she held her hand up to feel the slow trickle of blood that had started. "Do the next hook now."

He did as she ordered, and placed the opposite hook in the skin of her shoulder. The girl was taking this all in surprisingly well. She was screaming of course, but he imagined that if it were him, he would have already passed out from the pain. "Pull her up!" Bathory ordered.

Jared yanked on the chain that raised the device up in the air above the tub. Elizabeth scooted on her butt to position herself underneath the girl. The blood was trickling all over her body now, and she raised her head up towards it, opening her mouth in pleasure. "We'll need more hooks," she called out to Jared.

"Where shall I place them?" he asked, nervously.

"Just a few inches under those hooks. On her ribs. There are several more hooks, so leave plenty of room," she explained, as she lavished in the blood.

Jared had placed the additional hooks into the girl's skin, cringing every step of the way. He thought loyalty to Bathory would earn him something, but never this. He did not want this disgusting position. Elizabeth had him place two more sets of hooks, and with each new placement the girl got weaker. Finally, she passed out from either the pain, or the blood loss.

As Jared was putting in yet another set of hooks, the doors to Bathory's room flew open, and in flew the dark fae Prince, Rex. Bathory was shocked, and angry at his unannounced arrival.

159

"What ever happened to knocking?!" she exclaimed, as she stood up in the tub, ducking to avoid hitting her head on the body hanging above her.

Rex moved over to her, and embraced her in a rare moment. "I wanted to apologize for earlier. I was not myself, and was having a bad day," he explained, trying to convince her the aggression towards her was not like him.

Bathory believed him, as he raised her out of her bloodbath, and placed her gently onto the floor in front of him. She looked longingly into his otherworldly eyes. "Rex, my dear. It is perfectly fine! What are you even apologizing for?" she asked him, already lusting for another taste of his blood.

He smiled down at her with sincerity. "What does your heart desire tonight?" he asked her. "What can I do to make it up to you?"

Elizabeth's eyes flitted over to the body that was convulsing on the hooks above the bathtub. "Sit with me, and enjoy the show?" she asked shyly.

"As you wish," Rex replied, as he led her by the hand back into the tub that was soaked in blood now.

Before he sat down, he caressed a tiny crystal that his sister had given him earlier to let her know that he was with the Countess.

That was all that was needed to put things into motion. Rex put his lips to Elizabeth's in a convincing manner that turned his stomach. Telling himself over and over again, that he would only have to endure this for a few moments got him through the disgust of tasting the blood in his mouth. Bathory was in the moment, and he encouraged her to bite into him.

She squealed out in pleasure. "Rex! I have never had both your blood, and a human like this before! It is intoxicating! I just may regain all my strength in one sitting, I am so excited!" she said as her hands moved down to Rex's crotch. He moaned out in pleasure as she caressed his manhood.

He knew that he needed to get her fully distracted, so he reached up and ran his fingers through one of the many areas of blood that dripped down from the human body above them. Rubbing it onto his chest, and then sticking his fingers in her mouth, he whispered into her ear, "*I want you,*" softly.

Bathory moaned as she sucked on Rex's blood-covered fingers. She spread her legs willingly, and he entered her. Jared stood on the side, watching uncomfortably. Unsure what to do, he just blended into the shadows, and watched as his master made love to a dark fae.

Elizabeth tried to accelerate the sex, but Rex slowed her down. Being covered in blood, and slipping all over the bottom of the tub was pissing him off. But he kept his poker face on. He kissed her lips softly, even biting her bottom one as he told her "Slow down. I want to enjoy this."

It was as if all of her dreams had come true for Elizabeth. She had a human victim, tortured and hanging above her, while her Prince ravaged her. Closing her eyes, she leaned her head back against the tub, moaning in pleasure as Rex took one of her breasts into his mouth.

She was so distracted by the rhythm of the sex, the blood from the girl, and Rex's magical blood, that she didn't even hear the commotion downstairs. Elizabeth was in Heaven, but it would soon turn into her Hell.

She eventually heard the screams. Rex was still inside of her, pumping away, when her eyes popped wide open. "Did you hear that?" she asked him.

"No? Hear what?" he replied. He quickened the pace of his sexual ravishment on her.

She moaned out in pleasure for a moment, then put her bloodied hand on his chest to stop him. "You don't hear that?" she asked him once more.

He waited until he knew for certain that his sister, and her friends were in the house before he replied. "Yes! We are under attack! Quickly! To the window!"

They stood up, and bashed their heads on the girl hanging from the hooks. Shoving the body aside, Bathory barked out to Jared to open the gigantic window in her room. He did as he was told, as Rex stood by the door guarding it.

His Captain, Valentina, rushed up to the door, calling out from the other side. "Prince Rex! Are you alright?! We are under attack!" He opened the door and let her in. She had a sword at the ready, bless her beautiful heart, with the only arm that she had left.

Bathory was in a panic. Not yet back to her full self, but able to wield some magic after drinking blood, she tried her best to summon a protection barrier on the door.

"Don't waste your energy! Let us get you out of here, before it's too late!" Rex yelled out to her. Valentina shoved Elizabeth out the open, second story window, naked and all. The two of them flew down to catch her before she could even land.

"Quickly! I will open a tear! We shall get you to The Gloom!" Rex assured her.

Just as he said it, Skyy came around the corner, with her hands lit up. Elizabeth had never been more terrified in all of her long years.

# Chapter 17

The scene that we encountered when we got onto the property of the mansion was pretty much what we expected. The moment we hit the ground, Rex's dark fae fulfilled their end of the bargain. They either subdued, or killed, any vampire on the lower levels. The upper level, was of course reserved for the One & Only Elizabeth Bathory. Nobody went up there, unless called for. Just as planned, the one-armed dark fae "Captain" that I hated so much, Valentina, flew up to assist Elizabeth and her Prince, Rex.

We instructed the dark fae to leave Claude untouched. He would suffer after all of the major action went down. For now, he got to watch all of the remaining vampires get slaughtered. Once I knew Valentina was upstairs, I exited the mansion, and ran to the backyard, where they would be escorting Bathory to safety.

As I turned the corner, I summoned my ball of magical sunlight. The look on Bathory's face was priceless, and I wished that I had a camera to capture it. Rex and Valentina did a convincing job that they were helping her, and for all I knew maybe they were. Sergei and Lucius followed closely behind me, with their fire at the ready. Aiden rushed up next to me, even though the heat from my magic made him uncomfortable. Christian, Flavia, and Fiona were perched on the rooftop of the mansion, and he shot arrows down in the grass around Bathory, conveniently missing her.

The Divine Assassins were instructed to find Arabella and Aimee. Ridley was a nervous wreck going into the mansion, not knowing what we would find. The lower level was cleared, and there was no sign of them there, so as we moved outside, they moved up to the second floor.

Rex, Valentina, and Bathory took off running into the woods behind the mansion. She was naked, and covered in blood...and I could smell it from here. It was Aimee's blood, which wasn't a good sign. It was also on Rex's body, and I wasn't sure what to think of that either. I pretended to fall back a little bit, to give them enough of a gap to let Rex do his thing. If they screwed us over, we would lose Bathory.

Bathory kept looking behind her to see if we were still following. She was starting to slow down. The blood she drank only gave her strength for a short time, from what we had gathered. "Hurry up! Open the tear!" she screamed out, just before she tripped and fell onto her hands and knees.

Rex stopped, while Valentina helped her up. He began to cast his magic, as beautiful illuminated clouds of purple and deep blue began to form around him in the air. "Faster!" she yelled out. We ran up on them right as the tear to The Gloom was opened.

Valentina shouted out "Go! Hurry!" and shoved Bathory through the portal first. Rex went after her, and Valentina signaled to us to follow as she jumped through and disappeared. Looked like they were holding their end of the bargain up.

"You don't have to go in, Skyy. We can witness this for you," Aiden reminded me, for the billionth time. We had had this discussion over and over in the last few hours.

"I know Aiden. But you know I have to see this through."

Lucius and Sergei jumped through the tear before Aiden and I did. "Let's go," I said, and took Aiden's hand.

What Bathory managed to miss in her panicked run to "safety" was Dreamer and Solara in their light-forms up in the trees opening a tear to The Lucent. Rex's "magic" was all for show.

Within seconds, we emerged into The Lucent. As expected, the overly bright sunlight would have an effect on me, but I would tough it out as long as I could. It was worth it. Bathory was on her knees, begging Rex for help. He was also on the ground, screaming out in agony, with Valentina next to him. Bathory's skin was smoking from the sunlight, as she tried her best to summon any kind of magic that might buy her a few extra moments. She still didn't put two and two together, and thought this was some kind of mistake. "Rex, we must get back through the tear!" she moaned out, crawling on her belly towards the portal back to our own dimension.

Rex was in far more agony than Bathory was. His dark, inky skin was actually igniting in flames in certain spots. His magical tattoos were disappearing, and floating up into the sky like glittering ash off of his body. He was in so much pain, that he couldn't speak. Valentina was in the same boat.

Dreamer flew through the tear behind us, with one of their leaders, a Lucent fae we all knew and respected, named Solara. Dreamer's face scrunched up in sadness as she watched her brother writhe in agony before her. "Go to him," Solara told her, and Dreamer flew over to him instantly. Putting her tiny hands on his back, she began speaking in another language.

I was getting weaker, and fainter by the moment in the intense sunlight of The Lucent. Light was amplified here, much more than it was in our own dimension. We had been inside for less than thirty seconds, but it felt like an eternity. The other vampires were perfectly fine, with their sunlight protection spells that the Divine Assassins performed on them.

Knowing I had to act fast, I gathered all my strength, and walked over to Bathory. Her skin was melting off her body, and you could see straight to the bone in spots. "There are no phylacteries here, Bathory," I laughed at her, as I lit my hands up with my sunlight. Her black eyes were begging me for mercy. She could no longer speak from the immense pain she was in. The sunlight of The Lucent would kill her soon enough, but I wanted to be the one who would deliver the final blow.

"My family, and the world will finally be rid of you," I yelled out, as I launched a ball of magic towards her. She was disintegrated into nothing in the blink of an eye. Though it was gratifying beyond belief, it took everything out of me, and I collapsed to my knees.

"Solara! Please, get Skyy back to our own world!" Aiden called out as he gathered me up in his arms. The Radiant fae nodded, and opened a tear up once more. Aiden ran through it, as the others followed closely behind.

Shortly after we got back, I passed out. When I woke up, we were inside Bathory's now-empty mansion. I was on a couch on the lower floor. "How long was I out?" I asked.

"Almost an entire day," Aiden replied, smiling at me. I could tell from the look on his face that he was worried sick over me.

Shooting up on the couch, I exclaimed, "A day?! What has happened in the time I have been out? Where is Aimee and Arabella?"

Aiden put his hands on my shoulders to calm me down, and to keep me from standing up too quickly. Christian, hearing I was awake, entered the room and handed me a mug of blood. "Hey you," he smiled at me.

"Hey. So fill me in please," I said, as I sipped on my blood. "Tell me Bathory is truly dead, and I didn't dream it?"

"Nope, you didn't dream it, she is super-dead. You barbecued her," Christian said, as he laughed.

Nodding my head as I continued to drink my blood, Aiden filled me in on the rest. "Arabella is fine, we found her locked in a dog cage upstairs in Bathory's suite. Aimee on the other hand, was in very bad shape when they found her. Bathory had almost killed her, if they had gotten to her even five minutes later, I think it would have been too late," he informed me.

"Where is she now?! Is she okay?" I asked, worried for her.

"Ridley is with her, they took her back to Lucius' villa in Italy to recover. We had no choice but to turn her. She had extensive damage to her spine, much like Christian did. Arabella told us Bathory hung her from some torture device, where the Divine Assassins found her still hanging, unconscious. Her ribs, and back were broken in multiple places, along with other damages that were about to kill her," Aiden continued.

Gasping, I put my hands to my mouth. "Oh my God!" Did Ridley see her like that?"

Christian and Aiden both nodded. I couldn't imagine the scare that must have been for Ridley. "Lucius offered to turn her,

166

and acted immediately after Ridley gave him the approval," Christian told me.

"Wow. This certainly isn't the path I wanted for Aimee and him. But at least she is alive. What about Rex and Valentina? Have you heard from Dreamer?"

"We have not had any contact from them. I assume that is their own business. Rex knew what he was signing up for when he offered to do it. Though I have no love for the dark fae, sacrificing himself for the better of the world was a valiant thing to do," Aiden said.

Finishing off my cup of blood, I nodded. "Indeed. I will check in with Dreamer soon to find out what has been going on in The Lucent since we left. And Claude?" I asked, wanting to know what became of my enemy.

"He is still where you asked us to leave him. We've been guarding the mansion tightly, killing off any stray vampires who come wandering around checking in for the Bathory cause. We knew how important it was for you to be the one who killed him, as well as Bathory," Christian grinned at me.

"You are all awesome. Thank you so much for helping me with this. I know you didn't want me going to The Lucent, Aiden, but it was something I had to do. Bathory had personal ties to my family, my ancestors. She ruined so many lives. I had to be the one to kill her. Speaking of family, is Grandpa okay?"

Christian nodded once more, "Yep, he's just fine. He heard what you did, and grinned like a schoolboy. He's so proud of you."

I looked down at my hands, and noticed they were glowing even more than before. The sunlight in The Lucent probably supercharged my powers. Hopefully Ridley and the Divine Assassins could figure out how to hide my hands and eyes when I wanted to go out in public. Sighing, I swung my legs onto the floor and sat up on the couch. "Well, we have a few visits to make. And since we're already here, Claude will be first up," I said, as I stood up and brushed my pants off.

As soon as I said that, I heard his heartbeat pick up from the across the mansion. He knew I was coming. Good. We walked into the area he was being held, and I smiled at him. He was sitting upright in a chair, bound by silver chains, which took away his ability to talk, or move. But I could see the terror in his eyes. He was blood-starved, and I wondered when the last time he had fed was.

Walking dramatically around him to stand behind him, I greeted him. "Hello, Claude." Tapping my fingers on the back of the chair, I could feel the tension coming off of him. "I'm glad my friends saved you for me. I had to take care of your Master first, and all of the others that were working with your little cause. I told you that you picked the wrong side, didn't I? You didn't think we were capable of winning the war? Well, guess who looks stupid now?" I mocked him.

Moving in front of him, so I could see his eyes, I snapped my fingers and summoned my magic. His heartbeat increased even more, and it sounded as if he were running a race now. I toyed with him, summoning, and extinguishing my magic over and over…keeping him guessing when I would finally kill him. It was quite fun, but I knew we had more important matters to attend to, like Aimee, so after playing around with him for over ten minutes, I finally walked over to Claude and put my hand on his shoulder. He disintegrated in seconds, and that was that. "Good riddance, you slime ball," I whispered, to nobody in particular.

"What should we do with the mansion, now that this is all taken care of?" I asked Aiden.

"I don't want there to be any chance of others picking up where Bathory left off. We should keep some Divine Assassins here on duty for the next few weeks, to make sure any who come knocking are taken out. Will your grandpa approve of that?" he questioned me.

"I am sure he will. With Bathory, and Jack gone, the Divine Assassins will have a lot more free time on our hands. I'll talk to him right away," I told him. Pulling out my phone, I made the call. He was more than happy to keep some men on site, and praised me over and over again for my hard work.

Before we hung up he added in, "There is one more thing, Skyy. We examined the house from top to bottom, and found what we believe to be another book of souls that she was beginning to create. I had the men take it back to headquarters, where we will perform the same ritual as before, to hopefully release the souls."

It didn't shock me to hear it, as that was her biggest source of power before we killed her the first time. "Be careful. If you need my help, let me know and I'll portal over to headquarters."

"You be careful too, Skyy. We'll talk soon," Grandpa said, as we hung up.

"Now that we have that taken care of, I want to go check in on Aimee, Ridley, and Arabella. I'll open a portal." Taking Christian through first, and coming back for Aiden, we landed in Italy at Lucius' gorgeous villa. It was quite odd that Aimee was also making her transition into a vampire here, in the very same room as I did. Lucius rushed over to me when he saw me emerge.

Embracing me in a hug, he looked me over to make sure I was okay. "Skyy, my girl. You are going to give us all a heart attack one of these days. I am glad to see you're awake," he smiled at me. Flavia was right behind me, also giving me a huge hug.

"Welcome to my daily life," Aiden said, with a chuckle. I knew that I constantly had him worried, and hoped that now that all of our enemies were taken care of we could settle down into a more stable life.

Swatting him on his arm gently, I assured everyone that I was fine, and thanked them for their help. All of my vampire friends were at the villa, and were very happy to see me. Arabella, still looking shaken up, joined the room as well.

Smiling at her, and giving her a hug, I asked how she was doing. After exhaling a long breath of air, she answered me. "Well...it's been rough. I am still trying to process everything that happened, but thank my lucky stars that I am still alive. If it wasn't for you guys, I would be either dead, or tortured for eternity at the hands of that madwoman."

"We are just glad we got to you both in the nick of time," I replied to her, smiling. I knew that Arabella had been through hell and back in the short time she had known us, but I hoped that she knew we would always be there for her now. Even Lucius, who she used to be terrified of, was coming around. He placed his huge hand on her slight shoulder, and pat her in reassurance that everything would be just fine. She looked up at him, and gave him an awkward smile. She excused herself shortly after that, and Fiona went with her to keep her company.

"Can we go check in on Aimee now?" I inquired. Lucius nodded, and led the way to the familiar room that I transitioned in. Memories came flooding back to me, as he knocked on the door. Aiden and I walked quietly into the room, and Lucius shut the door for us and walked back down the hallway to give us privacy.

Sergei was also in the room, guarding Ridley for when Aimee woke up from her transition. Ridley hadn't slept much, if at all, that much was apparent. His normally perfectly groomed appearance was disheveled, and he had huge dark circles under his eyes. I glanced at Aimee, who was sleeping peacefully. She looked perfectly fine, and was transitioning normally from the looks of it. Walking over to Ridley, I gave him a long, silent hug. He hung on to me for a very long time, before burying his head into my stomach from his seated position and crying. Sergei silently left the room, to give us all privacy.

"I'm so sorry, Ridley. At least we could save her." I whispered, as I pat his back. I could tell Aiden was uncomfortable at the sight of another man crying, but he knew the deep love that Ridley had for Aimee. Ridley continued to sob for several minutes, letting all of his stress and emotion flow out. Finally, he let me go, and wiped his eyes. Aiden handed him some tissue that was next to the bed on a night stand.

"I didn't want this for her. All I wanted was to keep her safe. It is all my fault, I should have listened to you, Skyy. You told me to let her go, and I didn't. And now she is here, turning into a vampire," he said, beating himself up as he stared at her body.

"Ridley, the past is the past, we can't do anything about it. You can't blame yourself for caring about her. At least we got there in time to help her. I know this isn't what any of us wanted for her, but she is alive, and she'll recover just fine. You two can go on to have a great life together," I assured him.

"You should have seen her. When I walked into the room, she was hanging from the roof on hooks and chains. They were all over her body. Blood was everywhere. The smell was horrifying. I vowed to myself that I would never let Bathory kill another person I loved after she took my mom and sister. She almost took Aimee from me as well. I thought she was dead. It was the worst sight I have ever seen. I will never get the image out of my head." He went on to explain the horrible story to us.

Putting my hand on Ridley's hand, I continued to listen to his story of how they found her, and turned her. It was awful to hear, but I kept reminding him that she was safe now, and that Bathory was dead. We sat with him for several hours, waiting for Aimee to wake up, until finally she did.

Gasping for air, she sat up in the bed, confused. Her crystal clear, blue eyes, were glowing brightly, getting more intense as the seconds passed. Ridley's immediate reaction was to run to her side, but Aiden quickly restrained him. "Careful! She is blood lusting after waking up, Ridley. Stay back." Instead, I ran over to her bedside, and took her hand to comfort her, and reassure her that we were there with her.

Fiona, hearing that Aimee had woken up, came rushing into the room with blood, just as she had when I woke up from my death-sleep. Handing me the mug, I helped Aimee take her first uneasy sips of what would become her source of all nutrition and nourishment from now on. Again, just like me, she was unsure about drinking the blood, but the moment it touched her tongue, instinct kicked in and she swallowed it in gulps. Fiona and Christian both kept the mugs of warm blood coming.

Ridley sat in the chair, with Aiden guarding him, worried sick. Aimee, finally sated from her initial bloodlust, glanced over at Ridley. Her eyes were still on fire, and her need for blood would not diminish anytime soon. "How did this happen? Who turned me?" she asked, confused about her new body. I could tell that she was scared it was Bathory who may have done it to her.

"Lucius did. You were on the verge of death, we asked Ridley for permission," I explained to her. Aimee looked over at Ridley once again, and gave him a shy smile.

"Bathory? What happened? I blacked out after a while. She was torturing me…the pain was too much to handle."

"She is dead, finally. Hopefully all the troubles that were caused because of her died along with her. A good chunk of the vampires that were either warring, or joining her cause also died, so New Orleans should be a safer place for your cousin," Aiden said.

It was a lot for her to take in, and she needed more blood. Fiona tended to her, and we asked to see Ridley outside. He hesitated, not wanting to leave Aimee alone, but knew that she was in good hands. He left the room with us, and Aiden and I took him on a short walk on the large property. "Ridley, this will be a very long, and hard journey for you, being a human. You're not going to be able to be near her for these first few weeks, if not months, and you're never going to be able to be fully alone with her for several years until she can control herself," Aiden explained, gently.

His brow furrowed, and he ran his hands over his cheeks that were growing light stubble from not shaving recently. I could see he was on the verge of crying again. "Ridley, you can do this. It's rough…even Aiden struggled at times with me before I transitioned into vampire, and he is hundreds of years old. But, if you love her, it's worth it," I told him.

His sadness turned into anger, and he yelled out into the wind loudly, balling his hands into fists. After that he collapsed to his knees. "I love her, Skyy. More than anything. After almost losing her, I can't not be by her side at all times. Turn me. Just turn me…make me into a vampire, so we can be happy together," he pleaded with us.

It shocked both Aiden and I, and we looked at each other in amazement. Ridley had his back to us, still on his knees in the grass. We were puzzled by his request, and didn't know how to reply. He spoke again, before we could answer. "Yes, I know how hard it is, and how much I would have to give up…but I have nothing without Aimee. Think of how it was for you Aiden…could you imagine a life without Skyy? I have nobody but my father left, and we have a strained relationship as it is. No friends, only Divine Assassins who are much older than me. Please, just turn me, I know the risks…the reward is much more important to me than mortal life," he said, trying to convince us again.

"I-I don't know what to say, Ridley," Aiden stuttered out. "You're right, I couldn't imagine a life without Skyy in it. You have been a part of the supernatural world for a very long time. You grew up hating vampires, hunting them. The hardest part of the transition for humans, is the shock of knowing there is a supernatural world, so I have no doubt you'd adjust fine there. But, becoming the thing you've always hated? Are you ready for that?"

"I never knew any better before I met you and your friends, Aiden. We were taught to kill them, and to hate them, because that is all they do to us humans. All the vampires we encountered were terrible to the core. Then, I met you, and my whole opinion changed. I know that if we become part of your bloodline, we'll always stay on the right path. With your help, we'll learn to live great lives as vampires," he said, smiling at the two of us, finally standing up.

"Well, I have no objections, Ridley. You're an adult, and you know what you're getting in to. I suspect it would be much easier for you and Aimee both, though no matter what, it won't be easy. You'll be together, but the first years are hard because of the blood lust. We'll have you stay with one of us until we're positive you can be trusted on your own," Aiden replied, letting him know the rules.

Ridley smiled, finally seeing some light in all of this dark tragedy. "There are some things I have to do before I could be turned. Magical wards, and implants to protect me from vampires that need to be removed. I can have it done by the end of the day," he said excitedly.

"Very well. Get your things in order, and I will be the one to do it myself, Ridley," Aiden told him.

We walked back to the villa, and he rushed to Aimee's room to tell her. She was still sipping on blood, but was overjoyed to hear his decision. I figured that she would argue with him about it, but she didn't bat an eye, and instead was thrilled. I think the idea of navigating her new world with the person she loved by her side, instead of on the sidelines, made her feel much more safe.

Ridley said goodbye to Aimee, and we opened a portal to meet with my grandfather. I went with him, to break the news to him together.

# Chapter 18

As expected, my grandfather still held on to his deep-rooted hatred for vampires. Though he was coming around to the idea of me, and my friends, he still could not fathom why someone would *choose* to become a vampire. "Ridley, this idea is ridiculous. The men already have a hard enough time accepting Skyy into our ranks, they will have an aneurism over the thought of one of our long time members becoming one. Have you spoken to your father about this?" Grandpa probed him.

Ridley shook his head no. "My father doesn't have a say in this. You know our relationship isn't the best. Killian, sir, my mind is made up. I am not here to ask permission; I am here telling you that this is my plan. And I ask for your help in removing my wards," he boldly said. It took my grandfather back a little, as Ridley has always been a quiet, soft-spoken, dutiful member of the Order.

"Well then, I guess that is that. Yes, I will help you. I am not happy about your decision, but I know my granddaughter will take good care of you. It is hard, in my old age, to come to terms with vampires actually being decent. I mean no offense to you Skyy. I rather like Aiden and your crew, but old feuds are a hard thing to overcome." Grandpa thought on things for a moment more, than stood up and guided Ridley to another room.

"We're going to need a few more men in here for this, because once the wards and magic are gone from him, your urges to feed off of him will increase. For his own safety, I'll ask you to stay in the far corner of the room, and once we are done we will port him back on our own," he explained.

Once the other Divine Assassins were in the room with us, Grandpa started his ritual. The magical spells, that were invisible to me before, began to glow on Ridley's skin. His neck, arms, hands...all of the visible skin, started to glow with odd symbols. Soon, the symbols rose up off his skin, and vanished. "We have two vampire ward implants inside of you that need to be removed as well," Grandpa said as he got a tool similar to the one they tried to use to implant me. An odd looking screwdriver zipped into his skin, quickly removing the microscopic implants from him. Grandpa tossed them into a glass jar that held a blue colored liquid, which sizzled when the implants hit it.

Placing two Band-Aids on his incisions, Grandpa wiped his hands off on his pants, and pat Ridley on his back. "That's that, Ridley. I have to say, I am going to miss you around here for the time being."

Ridley stuck his hand out to shake Grandpa's. "Sir, thank you so much for your help, and it was a pleasure serving under you, and learning from you. If you guys ever need me, I am a call away."

The men took Ridley back to Lucius' villa, where I knew Aiden would take care of him until I returned. Grandpa wanted a word with me before I left. He offered a chair to me, and I sat down in it. "Skyy, I know that things have been hectic for you lately. Once again, I couldn't be prouder of you for taking on Bathory like you did. You need to take some time, help Ridley and Aimee, and get yourself settled in to your new world. With Bathory gone, the Divine Assassins can focus on other things, like learning, and scribing down new spells, and cataloguing the events that happened with the demise of Bathory. No doubt, we will still hunt vampires, but our major threat, the reason our Order was formed in the first place, is finally gone. All thanks to you. I want you to take some time off, go be young and happy. We'll always be here if you ever need us, and if we need you, of course we'll call on you," he told me.

I nodded to him, and smiled. "Thank you, Grandpa. I was more than happy to help, though my new-found powers were probably why I was as eager as I was."

"Don't fool yourself, Skyy. You're a Huntington…you've got bravery in your bones. If you see your parents anytime soon, make sure to give them an extra hug for me. I sure do miss them. Now go on, dear one. Get back to your husband. But you better keep in touch," he ordered me, with a serious look on his face.

I hugged him tightly, and thanked him for everything. "I love you, Grandpa. See you soon."

We waved goodbye one last time, before I opened my own portal back to the villa. As soon as I was on the property, Ridley wanted to know when we could start the transition. Aiden called for Lucius, who had prepared another room for the event to take place in.

"You are free to use this room. I'll leave you to it. And, welcome to the family Ridley," Lucius said, smiling at him.

"Thank you for your kindness, Lucius," he replied. Lucius gently closed the door behind him, as Aiden and I were left in the room alone with Ridley. Grandpa was right, the urges to drink from him were much worse than before his wards were removed, but I fought through it, and knew Aiden would never let me hurt him.

"Get yourself comfortable, and we'll begin once you're ready," Aiden informed him.

Ridley took his shoes off, and unbuttoned his shirt that he had on. He had a comfortable undershirt on beneath it, and kept that on. He took off his belt, and emptied his pockets before letting us know he was all set. "Okay. This is it I guess."

"It's easier if you lay on the bed," Aiden said, gesturing to the bed.

I stood in the corner, watching every single detail. Aiden made sure Ridley was comfortable, then bit into his wrist. Ridley flinched in pain, and Aiden took over his mind to ease the pain. Ridley closed his eyes as Aiden sucked on his wrist for a few moments. The smell of his blood was overwhelming, and I fought every urge I had to jump on top of him and drink along with Aiden. Soon, Aiden bit into his own wrist and put it up to Ridley's mouth. The first few drops hit his lips, and he flinched at the taste of it. Then he placed his mouth on the open wound and drank as much as he could tolerate, gagging the whole time.

Within seconds, his eyes closed, and he went into his death-sleep. The wound on his wrist healed up quickly, and we could do nothing but wait now. All of us took turns waiting on him to wake up, and it took only about eight hours. He emerged from his death-sleep just like Aimee and me before him…hungry. His eyes were on fire, and we had blood ready for him immediately. Once he was able to speak, he asked how long it had taken.

"Eight hours. You did well," was Aiden's reply.

I smiled at him, no longer having any cravings for his blood, which was a nice change. "So…does this make you sort of like my brother? Or a son?" I teased him.

"You brat," he laughed, and tossed a pillow over towards me. "You're still my partner in crime, and I suppose that you're my best friend. That'll have to do."

"You're stuck with me for eternity now!" I stuck my tongue out at him. Ridley wanted to drink up as much as he could, so he could gather up the strength to see Aimee.

"Will we be able to be together while we continue through the next few days?" he asked, hopefully.

We both nodded at him. "Yes, you can stay in the same room, be together…whatever your heart desires," Aiden told him. At that news, he smiled. We kept him in his bed for a little while longer, as he gained his strength back with the never-ending supply of blood.

Finally, it was time to take him over to Aimee's room. She jumped off the bed and flew into Ridley's arms. She looked so much better than when we left her the last time. I was so happy for the two of them, and knew that their life together would be great. We left them to their reunion, closing the door behind us.

We found Lucius, and informed him that we were taking some much needed time alone, and would be back later on in the evening to check on our new vampires. Opening a portal back to our mansion in Massachusetts, we stepped through together, hand in hand. We landed in the home it all started in. It seemed like so long ago, that Aiden took me here to protect me from the first wave of Bathory's minions.

The house was dark, and quiet. Aiden flipped on the first light switch we came across, and the memories came flooding back to me. I closed my eyes, and breathed in the familiar scent of the house. Of Aiden's bath soap, the familiar scent of his clothes. We were home again, and it felt wonderful. With Bathory gone, we could take up residence here once again. Though, was this really what I wanted? To go back to my old life? That would have to be something I would need to think on. But for now, it felt right, and it felt comfortable. All that was missing was my sweet dog, Cupcake. She was living a happy life with Lucius' dogs in his villa. Now that I knew we were safe, we could bring her back with us.

"Shall we, milady?" Aiden asked, as he took my hand and guided me up the staircase that led up to his amazing bedroom.

"We shall," I said, as he surprised me by picking me up and carrying my up the stairs. We spent hours in the giant bed together, before taking a long, hot bath in his luxurious Jacuzzi tub.

We dined on some blood by the fireplace in his room, lounging on a soft rug as we dried off from our bath. Aiden brushed out my long, wet hair as I leaned back into him. "Well, we have a lot to take care of from here on out. Four new vampires, along with you. They will need all the support we can give them, and since Ridley is the closest with you, I think we should offer to let them stay with us until we can be sure they are able to be on their own," Aiden suggested.

Sipping on my blood, I nodded my head. "I agree. I'd love it if we could all stay on the same property...the whole family...and take care of one another for a few years. Spread things out, of course, for privacy, but keep us close. What do you think?"

"I was thinking the very same thing. Lucius and I will go over our properties, and see which ones can accommodate that. With Flavia still trying to adjust back into this new, modern world, she will need the support from you ladies. Same with Arabella, who needs friends now more than ever. She has nobody, and I can't imagine how hard this has been for her. Christian has Fiona, of course, and he is transitioning better than anyone I have ever encountered. And we'll keep an eye on

Aimee and Ridley. Sergei will probably stay on to help for a while as well. It'll be fun," Aiden laughed.

"I wouldn't have it any other way. I have the perfect life. The man of my dreams, and the best friends anyone could ever ask for. Thank you so much for standing by my side, Aiden."

I turned my head up to kiss him, and he whispered, "I'll never be anywhere else than by your side, milady. I love you."

## THE END

# Epilogue

Dreamer held on to her unconscious brother's body for so long, she lost track of time. They both knew the risk they were taking when they decided to help Skyy, and to rid both of their worlds of Bathory's grasp once and for all.

When she first came through the tear, she screamed out at the sight of her dark fae brother burning up in the light of Her Splendor. She was given permission to go to him, and she took his hand as she watched his skin ignite. He was in so much pain; he couldn't even respond to her when she asked what he needed to comfort him.

Her dear friend, Holland, was trying her best to comfort the one-armed Captain, Valentina. It seemed nothing they could do would help. Dreamer knew better than to use her healing magic on a dark fae, it would just amplify his agony. She sat by his side, even as his dark flesh melted off onto her, burning her own legs in the process. Her light, iridescent skin, looked so pale compared to his inky, skin. His shimmered, but as if it were water in dark, black oil. Dreamer's shone like a pearl.

It took several hours before the dark fae finally went unconscious. The flesh had been burned off of his body. His dark magic tattoos were seared off by Her Splendor. What was left in Dreamer's lap now, was the muscles, viscera, and bones of her brother. Glistening in the light of Her Splendor, the sticky blood stayed fluid, and did not congeal. Holland held what was left of Valentina, who was in the same condition.

The two of them sat vigilantly, for three days. Dreamer cried so many tears, she was afraid that there were none left to cry. She missed her brother so much. All she could do now was wait, and hope.

Finally, Rex began to twitch. It started out slowly at first, then the twitches became stronger, and he began to move his muscles. Still skinless, she knew that it was very painful for him to do so. His eyelids had been burned off in the process, but the first thing Dreamer did was look to her brother's eyes. Where they were once filled with hatred, they were now filled with love. She could see the darkness had been purged. They were no longer dark, and calculating, but a bright blue color.

Valentina awoke shortly after Rex did, and Holland cried out, "It worked!" Dreamer's eyes filled with tears.

She cradled Rex's head in her delicate hands, as tears dropped down onto his body. Soon, he was able to smile up at her. The process took many, many hours, but Dreamer and Holland took care of their patients and watched in awe as their once dark, inky skin grew back. They were now covered in the same, pale, iridescent skin that all of the Radiant fae had. Rex's wings, which were once dark red, blue, and purple, were back to what they were when he was still among them: vibrant green and yellow. His eyes were shining like a bright blue sapphire.

Rex finally got the strength to stand up on his own two legs. He spread his wings out, testing them. He embraced his sister in a massive hug. "Thank you, sister. For watching over me, for never giving up on me, for loving me unconditionally. This was a huge risk for both of us to take, not knowing what would happen. Perhaps we can save our people now," he said.

"Indeed. We must tell Mother right away! She will be thrilled to see you!" Dreamer squealed out.

Rex's attention went over to Valentina. She was not yet able to stand on her feet, but he looked upon her with love and admiration. She looked just as he had remembered her, before the darkness took them. Her long, violet-colored hair looked radiant. Her translucent wings were glowing on the edges with the same violet color. Her eyes looked like amethysts, and sparkled in adoration for Rex. He walked over to her, still not comfortable enough with his wings to fly, and took her into his arms, helping her to her feet.

Valentina wrapped her one good arm around him, and held on tightly. She looked into up into the face of the Prince she longed so badly for. "We did it," she said, smiling at him.

"Yes, we did it! Thank you for walking with me on this journey, my love," Rex said, shocking her.

"My love?" she asked, questioning his statement.

Rex bent over and placed his lips on hers, kissing her softly. "Yes. My love. I have wanted to do that for a very long time. And now we are free to be together."

Tears streamed out of Valentina's eyes. She never in a million years imagined her life would turn out like this. Her heart had been corrupted so deeply by the magic of the powerful Being who took so many of The Radiant fae, that she never thought she could come back. But now, she was free of its hold. Her old life seemed a million years away. They were free of Bathory, and of The Gloom. And most importantly, she was free to be with Rex.

Dreamer let the two of them have their moment, then told them that they needed to be going. "We have so much to talk about! I instructed Mother to make ready a room for you, in the event that this plan worked. Shall we go into the town? Everyone will be so overjoyed!"

Rex and Valentina nodded at Dreamer, and followed her as they held hands.

In The Gloom, word spread quickly of the betrayal. Rex's father, the King of the dark fae, was the one who was tasked with going to Delvinon with the news. As expected, it didn't go well.

The powerful Being that all fae feared, boomed out into the gloomy skies "This will not do. Perhaps it has been too long since The Lucent has had a taste of what I can do."

# About The Author

Holly Hudspeth, best-selling Dark Fantasy/ Paranormal Romance author, lives in Texas. The Skyy Huntington series is an epic, fast-paced series that consists of four books: The Lie, The Countess, The Pursuit, and The Portal. Guided by Moonlight – Lucius' Story is a stand-alone Dark Fantasy novel based on a secondary character from The Skyy Huntington Series.

She takes pride on the fact that her series has something for everyone. There is magic, fantasy, alternate worlds, horror, undying love, plenty of action, and numerous supernatural beings…some of which are her own unique creations! It will keep you turning the pages wanting to find out what happens next.

Holly's passion for literature began from the first moment she learned how to read. She enjoys writing fantasy, paranormal, romance, and horror stories, and has also created short stories based on avatars she played in online video games such as Everquest and World of Warcraft. Holly also likes to put her own fictionalized twist on historical figures in her books!

In her spare time, Holly likes to play mmorpg's, collect comic books, go to renaissance fairs and comic cons, travel, garden, and spend time with her family and friends. She and her husband currently reside in Fort Worth, Texas with their young son Gavin, and their 4 dogs which are spoiled rotten.

Twitter: https://twitter.com/SkyyHuntington

Website: http://www.hollyhudspeth.com

This is the end of The Skyy Huntington Series from Skyy's point of view. Look for other stories in the future, including the fate of the all of the dark and light fae! Thank you all so much for being a part of this magical journey with me, and with Skyy! Stay up to date on my website www.hollyhudspeth.com